# The Irish Tale

By Dulene Cipriano

ISBN: 978-0-692-15764-0

*Author's Notes:*
The photographs were taken by and belong to the author.
This novel only starts out as non-fiction for the first page or so, and
conversations about the grandmother are also non-fiction; otherwise,
everything in this novel is fictional.

*This novel is dedicated to my grandma Zelda Milliken,*

*who loved Ireland; even though she never saw it with*

*her eyes, she saw it with her heart, and taught me*

*to do the same.*

# Chapter 1: The Arrival of the Stranger

I was a woman who was only in her early 30's. I had experienced enough of life to know something about life, but not enough to be jaded or reflective. Coming from a somewhat secluded cultural enclave in Indiana, USA, I still found many experiences in the world new, curious, and interesting. I had already seen a few places in the world. I had gone to Bogota, Colombia for a brief trip to see a friend and had experienced some interesting aspects of that place, including how the rains in the semi-tropical climate in the morning made the rest of the day in this mountain city refreshing; how you could travel a lonely mountain road and find a small place to eat and drink in the middle of nowhere surrounded by the darkness of night; and how, in fact, coffee served in Colombia was the best tasting in the world.

I had also spent 5 months teaching English in South Korea, but this had been cut abruptly short by the death of my grandmother. My Grandma Zelda had been my life. To write a story about her effect on my life would almost require an encyclopedic set, starting with the Advent, then proceeding with Baking, Care, Confidence, and so many other entries to detail everything she gave to my life… Hugs, Love, Talks, Time, Walks… Time just walking and talking… Walks just for the sake of being side-by-side, and then the observations about life and love that came from someone who felt life and love naturally, and not as a set of rules to impart.

Grandma Zelda had been deteriorating, but her death was a finality that was hard to bear. In my encyclopedia, this would be the Zenith entry, and it seemed, without any possibility of ever talking to her again, my life was on a decline. Perhaps everyone has had such a person that is the definition and memory marker of a large part of their lives and emotions. It seemed, for the few years after her death, that the positive growth of my life had ended. I wondered if there was anything left to explore. I took a job that was stable, well-paying, and had contemplated buying a home. But in the middle of my search for a home, something stopped me. Just as I was at the point of anchoring myself to one place for the rest of my life, something inside of me said "weigh anchor", and I decided to take my life in another direction.

My mother had given me some money from the inheritance she had received from Grandma, and said, "Spend this on whatever you want… A new computer, or… a trip somewhere."

While a computer would have been a practical, long-term purchase, I immediately set my sights on Ireland. It was the natural choice. My Grandma Zelda, being mostly Irish by her ancestry, preached the country as a religion throughout my childhood. To come away from those years of faith and conviction in the beauty of Ireland without forming some love and longing for Ireland myself would have been a sacrilege of my love for my grandma. I thought about how she had never gotten to see this country; it wasn't for lack of money, however, but for lack of opportunity – she had been married to someone who didn't like to travel. Yet, despite never having been there herself, she made me yearn to go there. Although I had personally always wanted to visit England because of my love of Victorian literature, my love of Ireland was stronger by its connection to my grandma; so, after arranging the trip details, I was on my way to Ireland to land in the Shannon Airport on a day in August when I was only 31 years old.

The flight was a peculiar one. I was sitting in a window seat, when halfway through the flight a young boy with wavy blonde hair sat in the aisle seat next to me. He buckled up and seemed vivacious; his body movements were happy and giggly, but not obnoxious. I looked at him, and he finally looked at me, with two amazingly blue, happy eyes. His mouth smiled, but he said nothing. I couldn't help but smile.

"Hello," I said to him.

"Hello," he said, blushing, really happy. I had no idea what he was so happy about, but I couldn't help but engage with him.

"So, is this your first flight?"

"My first what?" he said, looking at me curiously.

I wondered whether English was not his native language. "Flight," I said, making the gesture of an airplane. "Your first time in an airplane."

He looked at me with some confusion, then said with a chuckle, "Maybe. I guess so."

I was a little bewildered at his evasive answer, but he seemed so cute that I kept going.

"This is only my third time in an airplane to go somewhere," I said to him. "But it's my first time coming to Ireland."

His smile immediately turned to an innocent frown.

"That's not possible," he said, childishly.

I laughed at his pure-hearted churlishness. "It's not only possible, it's true. This is my first time to be in Ireland."

The boy's face became doubtful, then looked at me like I didn't know what I was talking about, then became thoughtful. He put his hand up to his little dimpled chin and seemed to think.

"Maybe you just don't remember being here before," he said, openly and innocently, and his smile returned.

I smiled inside myself and decided to humor him, because I didn't want to break his spirit.

"Yes, that could be," I said, and my answer seemed to satisfy him and his happy mood was fully restored.

I kept looking at him, and he continued looking at me, obviously interested in continuing this conversation.

"How old are you?" I said.

"Hmmm…." He seemed to need to think about this. "I am… Hmmm… 9 years old."

I laughed. "You forgot your age?"

He laughed out loud, and his voice tingled softly like a running brook. I had never heard such charming laughter before.

"So where are your parents?"

Again, the boy looked at me with a concerned face, then seemed to think. He got up and looked over his seat. He seemed satisfied by what he saw, and came back and sat down.

"They're in back of us. But they're sleeping. Sssshhhh," he said, with a sweet, mischievous look in his eye, his finger up to his lips. Before I could get up to take a look myself, he put his little hand on my arm, and I felt this strange sensation… like he was familiar with me. But I just laughed that off as the excitement of the flight. Then he quickly asked me a question.

"Ma'am, why are you coming back to Ireland?"

"Coming back?" I looked at him and laughed, amused at his insistence on this myth of my return.

"Well, I'm COMING to Ireland as kind of a pilgrimage."

"You mean a holy voyage?"

I was shocked at his ability to understand that, but he didn't know the meaning of airplane. I chuckled under my breath. "Yes, I guess you could say that."

"Tell me about it, Ma'am." And his voice was so serious, I looked at him. His eyes seemed somewhat remote for a second, then he became very intent. Suddenly I felt it was important to explain to this complete stranger why I was coming to Ireland.

"Well..." I had to think about this. I didn't want to upset this young kid with a sad story. "I guess I'm going because my grandma loved Ireland, and she would talk about Ireland all the time as I was growing up, as if that was her true home. What was funny, was that she had never been to Ireland, but she preached Ireland like a religion, maybe the only religion she had."

I stopped to make sure the young boy was following me, but the expression in his eyes seemed clear, and was encouraging me to continue.

"When I was a child, she would always sing these Irish songs when she was singing me to sleep, and there was something in how she sang these songs that bespoke a love for this place that was beyond all reason, because there was no basis in reality for her to have such a connection to this country. And yet, she expressed her love for it, and through her love, my love grew. I came to develop a connection for this remote place."

I sighed. "My grandmother died over 2 years ago, without ever getting to visit Ireland. I've missed her deeply. My mother gave me some money from her inheritance, and I used it to come here. It was all I could do for the woman who had meant the world to me… To make the trip that she could never make."

The little boy looked at me, barely blinking. "That's a beautiful notion, ma'am."

"And it's a true one," I said, a little put off by some kind of laughter in his voice.

"I'm sure, for you right now, it is."

I was a little surprised at this answer, because it was not as childish as it should have been, so I wanted to change the subject.

"You never told me your name."

"I didn't?" he joked. "So… What is my name? Take a guess." And he seemed to be waiting with a sincere expectation in his face.

"Well… Thomas?"

He rolled his eyes and smiled. "No, guess again."

"Rory? Sean? Andrew? Keegan? William?"

His head keep shaking with each guess, and I finally fell silent, weary of the game.

"I give up. What's your name?"

He looked very serious. "But you already know it."

"I'm sure I don't," I said, trying to correct the boy.

"You don't…" he said, seeming to ponder. "But you *did*."

I must have looked confused, because he smiled and patted my hand softly.

"And you will again. Just go to sleep, ma'am." And he patted me on my hand again.

I had to admit, that all of a sudden, I felt tired. I was still turned toward the boy, and he toward me. He started humming some kind of song really low, and for a 9-year-old, it sounded very soft, beautiful, yet haunting. My eyes closed as I drifted on the notes of his voice, then I fell asleep.

In that sleep, I had a strange dream of this young boy. I was walking through forests that I had never seen before, where the sunlight streamed through the trees and cast a misty, translucent light upon the earth and the rivers and streams that seemed to wind everywhere through the forest. I heard some playful laughter, and saw the boy up ahead. He was naked, and I was shocked. He was enjoying the waters in a particularly sparkling stream, taking them into his palms, raising his hands above his head, then letting the waters cascade down his young child's body. The sun glowed softly on the white of his skin, and his golden blond hair reflected the sun's rays. He paused as I came close. He seemed to have been waiting for me, by how he smiled when he saw me. I stopped several feet away from the bank of the stream. The boy was unabashedly unashamed of his nakedness, while I blushed, and found it hard to look at him.

He laughed. "Ma'am, there is nothing to be ashamed of here."

I found myself unable to respond. I just stood there, hesitating. He stretched out a hand to me.

"Come inside," he said.

When I didn't move, he bent down and took some water in his cupped palms, then walked toward me, his youthful blue eyes reflecting something beyond the sky. He walked up to within inches of me, and his gaze seemed to look inside me.

"Come in."

This was all he said. Then he reached up above me and released the water in his hands, and out of all proportion to the amount in his hands, it poured down upon me with the force of a waterfall.

I woke up with a sudden start, and felt the airplane landing with some strong jolts onto the landing strip. I had to get myself readjusted to the reality of my plane seat and the plastic surroundings of the plane's inside. I looked at the seat next to me, but it was empty. I wasn't sure where the boy had gone.

I got up and retrieved my carryon parcel, and waited in line for the people in the airplane to file out. I remembered the boy's parents, so I turned around to say hello and tell them how much I had enjoyed the conversation with their son. A middle-aged couple was standing there, which I thought was strange considering that boy was so young.

"Hello," I said to them.

They nodded a hello to me. "Welcome to Ireland," the man said, probably sensing I was a tourist by my American accent.

"I really enjoyed talking to your son," I said to them.

The two looked at each other with a strange expression, then the man spoke.

"Our son?"

"Yes, the little 9-year-old boy that sat with me for a while. He said his parents were sitting in back of me. That was you, right?"

They looked at the seats, then back at me.

"Yes, those were our seats."

"Well… What about your boy? He's…." I trailed off, because their facial expressions were very strange in reaction to my words.

"Ma'am, we have a son, but he's 20 years old. And he wasn't on this flight."

I decided to let the conversation drop before I appeared insane. I knew the boy must have been somewhere else on the plane, but decided not to bother looking for him.

Armed with just my canvas duffle bag, my purse, a map of Ireland and my Bed & Breakfast vouchers, I got in the compact European car I had rented and drove onto the open road. The green hills and rural countryside continued as my companion throughout my drive. It seemed that only occasionally did homes show up along the road. There were no big cities along this road, not even small towns – just green hills. I drove along, listening to Irish pop songs, feeling like the only person in the world. My first destination was an ancient home from the 16th century, a quaint yet spacious yellow house with a wall around it, and then encircled by Irish mountains. A polite woman – very polite – greeted me, and I found myself nestled in a beautiful room for the night, with red carpeting and pink decorations, and old furniture. The bed was firm, but I loved firm beds.

I had visited a medieval castle earlier that day, so by the time I arrived at the B&B it was dinner time. It was a simple late dinner, with just 2 other American guests and myself. The conversation was muted but polite, as the couple was kind, and for me everything was new… And as I said, despite being in my 30's, my perspective was relatively green. I had lived through experiences, but had not really experienced too much understanding of the world, even by that age. I had always managed to keep myself as more of an observer of life and one who pondered its curious ways, rather than immersing myself in it. Perhaps this is why my grandmother's death was such a shock; for the first time, life hit me with all the deeper effects of "experience and understanding", and I was still trying to process it mentally and emotionally.

After dinner, we sat in the host's living room for more conversation, and our host asked us if we wanted an Irish Coffee. I was more than eager to say yes, always being turned on by the word "coffee". When she came back and gave me the glass cup filled with warm liquid, I took a taste, and was overwhelmed by the taste of whisky. I didn't drink alcohol, so this flavor just hit me over the head. I wasn't sure what to do, because my host was so polite, too polite, and here I was, ready to refuse the beverage that she had carefully prepared for me. Despite the vows I had made to never indulge in alcohol, I was struggling with another sacrament – to never offend one's gentle host. After about a minute or two of looking at the coffee-tinged whisky in my glass (if there was coffee in that drink, I would never have known it), I went ahead and drank it. But as a compromise, I didn't smile, and I didn't compliment it. The conversation continued, and then I went up to the bed in my room. The room took on a very comfortable feeling at that point, and as soon as I lay down my head, my thoughts were no more.

The next thing I knew my eyes were opening to morning. It's probably rare to actually remember a night of sleep. I remember a few. I remember the first night I slept in a tent in a forest (well, I lay there wishing for the sleep that never came). I remember the most comfortable hotel room I ever slept in and how dark it was, and how I could see the city outside being blanketed with a gentle snow. There are some other select nights I remember, but this one I remember particularly for its lack of memory – I think it was the heaviest, soundest sleep I had ever experienced. When I woke up, my body was full of energy. I was intelligent enough to know where that sound sleep had come from. So, while I cursed the evil of spirits, I did take a moment to inwardly extol the benefits of Irish whiskey… and now it is disclosed in this story for everyone to know.

After washing and dressing I went downstairs and ate a true Irish breakfast – eggs, meat, bread with Irish butter, and this time 100% coffee. I enjoyed this breakfast, and all those eggs and meat filled me up for most of the day.

I thanked my host, and took my things outside to my car. I looked around at the Irish morning, and it was just like all the times my grandma had sung about it… Fresh, open-hearted, and the colors of green and gold. It was like the angels' chorus – I felt my soul opening up to the wide-open spaces and the golden sun on the hills. My eyesight took in all the tranquil beauty, and then I looked toward my car, and it seemed like the hills had taken some kind of human form. There, leaning against my car, was a man, a very Irish-looking man, whose wavy, honey-blondish brown hair and skin on his face and soft bare arms were absorbing the gold of the morning light, and it was emanating from him as a gentle warmth. His eyes were excruciatingly blue, but they were also soft. He wasn't smiling, but just kept looking at me, with a calm seriousness. I was a little surprised that he was here, out in this rural country, and I stood several feet away from him. He was wearing just a simple, soft white T-shirt and some loose jeans that fit him nicely, with a sweater slung over one of his arms.

"Hello," I said.

"Hello," he said, and smiled a little now.

"Um," I looked around, for some indication of what I should say. "Are you… Are you a gardener?"

He laughed. "Do I look like a gardener?"

Just by how he had said that, I knew I had to say no. I looked at him for a bit, because it was nice just to look at him. "Sooo," I drawled, in my American style, "That's my car."

"Yes, I know this," he said gently, with another hint of a smile.

"Okaaayyy," I said drawling again. "Well, do you need a ride somewhere?" I asked, expecting him to say no.

"Yes, I would love one, Miss" he said, and he patted the car a bit and motioned with his head for me to come over.

I was a bit shocked. I was always taught to never accept rides from strangers, a rule which I had broken several times in my life without repercussions, but this idea of giving rides to strangers – was there a rule about that? Sure there was, in America; but here in Ireland, on this summer morning where everything sang with an enchanting light, there was something reassuring about how this man was leaning on the car, looking at me, and then he gently patted the car like it was an old trusted horse.

God be with me, I thought to myself, as I went over to him.

I told him my name, then asked him what his was.

"My given name is Lucas," he said, taking my outstretched hand. His skin felt dry and soft, and his grip was very congenial.

"What's your last name?" I asked him.

"Are you going to be calling me by my last name, like 'Mr. so-and-so'?"

I hesitated. "Well… Probably not."

"Then we won't be needing it," he said, tilting his head a bit.

I wasn't sure why I did this, but his voice was friendly and soft, and invited more conversation. My travel in Ireland was just myself, so I figured a little time with a companion for conversation would be nice.

"Ok, go ahead and get in," I told him. I unlocked the door on the left, and he got in.

I got in on the right side. "I don't know if I'll ever be completely comfortable driving on the left side of the road, but I've done ok so far."

He laughed. "I'm sure you'll do fine on these Irish roads," he said, his voice full of friendliness. "The only thing you have to worry about is a stray sheep coming into your path, and that's not going to kill you."

We both laughed.

"And don't worry about me, I'm not going to be a nagging passenger," he reassured me.

"So, where are you going? I can take you there."

He stared out the windshield, then looked a little to the right toward me, but not directly at me.

"Where are you going," he said to me.

"Well… I'm planning to visit the Lakes of Killarney today."

He looked more directly at me, then put his hand to his dimpled chin, like he was thinking. "Well, Miss. That sounds like a beautiful place. Let's go."

I had started the car, but had not yet put it in drive. I sat there looking at my steering wheel, hardly even daring to turn my head. I suddenly realized that I had a travel companion. I felt this man's presence next to me. I looked at his smooth, muscular arms and felt the relaxed way he sat, no fidgeting, and with just a gentle expression on his face, and I felt that I was safe. I put the car in drive and we left together.

## Chapter 2: Dreamwalking in Killarney Forest

As we drove, I felt curious about this man named Lucas, who had so suddenly appeared and then inserted himself into my trip. As the scenery went past us, I kept trying to think what to say. What does one ask a stranger? The comment or question couldn't seem too trite, or too personal, or too ridiculous, which was impossible to gauge with a stranger. So I decided to reach for what ended up just being too obvious...

"Have you ever been to Killarney National Forest before?"

He laughed. "I don't think there's a part of Ireland I haven't been to, Miss. I've wound through all of her parts." He voice was really tender when he said this, and it made me tingle.

"Sooo," I said, a little shyly, "why do you want to go there again?"

He laughed his genial laugh again, as if what I had said had been humorous. Then he momentarily touched my arm very softly, as if he was trying to get my attention.

"Just because I've been there once or even twice...or let's say even a hundred times... or let's say more..." and here he paused as his fingers lingered on my arm... "doesn't mean I've fully experienced it."

This man seemed younger than me, maybe in his mid-20's, but he seemed older than me in years. I realized I didn't know anything about him. Yet, I wanted to listen to his voice. And what he had said just then... I was not sure if he was talking about the forest, or something else. But it felt like he was talking about the forest, so I could not figure out what he meant by "a hundred times or more".

Maybe he had visited this place a lot in the past. I decided to let ignorance be bliss.

"Where are you from, Lucas?" I asked.

"Of course I am from Ireland."

"No… I know that. I meant, what part of Ireland are you from?"

Again, he was smiling. "I see. America is such a wide country that you tend to divide your identity and cultures into regions. To be honest, Miss, I'm from Ireland, and no matter what part of Ireland that be, I'm still Irish, and I'm still part of her whole self. And there's your answer."

The landscape of Ireland passed by us as green and lush as ever, as I kept driving. As I drove, this man named Lucas started humming a song really low, and it fell on my ears like the movement of a deep river. I stopped speaking, and just listened to him.

Once we got to Killarney National Forest, I wanted to take one of those wagon rides around, so we bought our tickets and waited for the horse and wagon to arrive. Our wagon driver was a young, gregarious man who wanted me to sit up front with him. Even though Lucas was kind of a sudden companion, I still asked him if it was ok that I sat up with the driver.

"Of course, this ride is yours," he said, as he relaxed back in one of the wagon seats.

As we rode around, we met various other drivers, and my driver, in his own sweet, animated way, pointed to me and said to his colleague, "Look, I've got one right here," at which we laughed. At that moment, however, I felt an arm across my shoulder, and Lucas was leaning between us, with his other arm across the driver's shoulder, and he said to the driver, "No, this one is with me."

I thought about my driver's youthful face and crinkled up laughing Irish eyes; then I saw the face of my companion, there was a softness to his cheek, but some few days of growth to his facial hair along the bottom of his cheek. It was within just 2 inches of my face, and all I wanted to do was reach up and feel it in those few seconds, but instead I suppressed the urge. Before I could look away, Lucas turned his head toward me, and said something in a whisper, but I didn't catch it – I was looking too deeply in his eyes. I couldn't understand what he said, it didn't seem like English.

My driver and I continued to joke around during the ride, but I could feel the man behind me, just silently sitting and watching the trees, and I felt like I was missing something by not sitting back there with him.

After the ride, I had a snack for lunch, and kept looking at this man who was still a stranger but made me feel glad to be with him.

"What are you thinking, Miss?" he said. But by the way he subtly smiled I think he already knew what I was thinking.

"Well, I felt like that ride was ok, but… I'd like to go out again. And this time just enjoy the scenery more."

"I was thinking the same thing. We had a very jovial driver, but he's too young to know how to really enjoy the beauty of these parts."

"He's young? But aren't the two of you the same age?"

"I wasn't talking about age, Miss."

I found myself musing over the things this stranger said to me. I was older in age, but I was beginning to feel very naïve.

He got up and dusted off his loose jeans. "Let me see if we can find someone else to take us around the place for a little longer."

I wasn't sure how long he was gone, but when he came back I didn't notice him until his hand gently touched the top of my hand.

"Come on, Miss." And he waited for me to get up, then we walked together, our arms just barely touching each other.

We ended up in a wagon with an old man named Mr. Tagney, and he drove much more slowly. We were very fortunate, because we were the only ones in his wagon, and afterwards I wondered if it was because there weren't any other customers or because Lucas had paid for us to have a wagon to ourselves. We settled in the back of the wagon together, and then Mr. Tagney said, "How would you like it, folks?" and Lucas said, "Take her slow." And that's what he did.

We sat next to each other for a while, just listening to the quiet sound of the breezes winding around the park on their own, and watching the trees and lakes of Killarney Forest barely moving by us – it was like watching the rotation of the earth, and knowing it was happening, but not feeling the movement. If I had not had my watch, it would have seemed as if time had stood still. Then Mr. Tagney spoke.

"So, you are from America," he said, as if he was stating something he already knew.

"Well, yes," I said. And the peace whispered around us. All I could feel was Lucas's hand lying on my shoulder. Then Mr. Tagney spoke again.

22

"America is a beautiful country," he said, more as a confirmation, rather than a question.

The soft, green outlines of the forest and blue sky spoke more to me in this moment than my own country. "I guess," I said.

"You guess?" he said, a bit amused. "Well, I wonder if your guess be correct, from the way you hesitated there," he added.

"It's just there are some things about my country that aren't so beautiful," I said. "I guess I can't qualify the whole as beautiful when there are parts that are not so wonderful."

"Hmm… So what part do you not like?"

I continued staring at the forest, and said, "I guess one thing would be how some people walk so fast."

"They walk fast?" He stopped and looked around at me. "Can you explain this?"

"It's like… People walk fast to get somewhere. And you are trying to keep up with them, but they walk with intent, as if that destination was the most important part of this walk, and you just get left behind, wondering what part you really play in their lives. But… Well, I guess when it comes to walking, it was walking with my grandma that I loved the most."

"And why is that?"

And here I found myself divulging my heart to a complete stranger. "Well, she and I would walk to places, or walk to the bus stop, and it was always a slow walk, where she would tell me the details of everything we passed by, or talk about life, which required as slow a walk as possible. Then, if we were going to the bus stop, we would stand there and wait, and sometimes it was with more conversation, but it could also be with silence. Our walks were always side by side, and sometimes we stopped, and I enjoyed just standing next to her. I also remember looking at the details of the places around us. I never seemed to miss anything with her."

"I can understand that," he said, as he continued driving at the slowest of paces.

"I can remember a time when I was on my way to somewhere or something important," he said.

"Where?" I asked.

"The where and the when are not mattering anymore now. It was many years in the past. I was heavy-footing it somewhere, and was intent on getting there, and I passed by some lass. But there was something in the way she was wearing her dress or walking that made me stop and turn around and take a more sincere look at her. Then I went from looking to walking back. And I stopped near her, and gave her a long gaze, and that was the end of me right there."

"You mean, the two of you fell in love and got married?" I said, curious to hear more of the story.

"Love, yes, there was love, but the details of this love are for a different story for a different customer. But the moral of this story is the value of slowing down, and giving yourself to the idea of stopping. Otherwise, there would be no story to tell."

"So, Mister," Mr. Tagney said, suddenly turning his attention to my companion, "What is it you do for your living?"

"I'm a singer," he said.

I was shocked out of my senses. I turned toward him in my seat, and he turned toward me. I realized just how much this man was a stranger to me, so I asked, "Where do you sing?"

"Here and there, all around Ireland," he said. And that was all he would say. I looked in his eyes, and noticed they were not the bright blue they had been at the wake of morning; instead, with the softer afternoon light filtering through the forest, his eyes were a tempered blue, and I felt very comfortable looking at him.

"If you don't mind…." And here I hesitated. If he were to refuse, it would make things feel strange between us. But I felt it better to ask. "Umm…. Could you sing a song for me?"

"For you…. Of course I can do that," he said. And as he seemed to be thinking what song to sing, he reached out and touched a strand of my hair and smoothed it back behind my ear. His own hair, thick wavy locks, just slightly moved in the breeze.

I was not prepared for his voice. Usually I just expect a normal voice, and hope that the person can sing in tune so I don't have to suppress my cringes. Most of the time the voice can sing the song, but it is a boring voice, even if it is a beautiful song. I was not prepared for what came out of this man. The voice, as he sang a soft lullaby-like song, came out soft, like cream on the tongue. His voice touched something inside me like the strains of a well-played violin, or piano, or a cello. It pulled at something inside of me. Something in his voice seemed to want something from me. Even though I was not familiar with this song, the lyrics did not matter…his voice made me cry without even thinking why I was crying.

Some days you want to forsake yourself
To leave all the bad memories behind
To be in that place of perfect peace

Where life was soft, laughter kind
You can have that with me
Let's take a walk together
In this place forever.
Listen to the breeze
It speaks to you
Listen to my voice
It's inside of you

When he had finished his song, I listened to the wind for a while, and I did hear something. But mostly, this man's voice had gotten somewhere deep inside of me. My body struggled with a feeling it had never had before. I thought about Mr. Tagney's story, his sudden encounter with love.

"Ummm… Lucas?" I said quietly.

"Yes, Miss," he answered dreamily, his fingers moving around on my shoulder.

"Do you have any love story to tell?" When I said this, I could see Mr. Tagney nodding. He couldn't help but speak.

"I'm sure he does. If you are human, you cannot help but have a story about love."

Lucas gazed at Mr. Tagney for a while, and was so silent and serious, that I started to wonder whether something was wrong. Even the old man looked back at us, wondering why there had been such a long pause. That's when my companion said something very curious to him.

"Love comes in all shapes and sizes."

Then he finally turned to me.

"Ay, Miss. I have a story." He moved very close to me, and put his arm around me, and his hand now lay on my other shoulder. He leaned into my ear and said softly, "And it's this one."

I was a little surprised and shaken, and I thought he meant me. Then he told an actual story.

"It was some time in the past. The time won't be mattering with my story, either. I gave the woman everything I had, and she found in me everything she needed, and she always found a way, in her own way, to give everything I had given to her back to me. I loved her beauty, and how strong and proud she could be, and she loved my steadiness, softness and playfulness. The sunlight and moonlight passed over us and through us for what seemed like millenniums, but we did not notice time; we were with each other, and we enjoyed each other's company, and needed nothing else. If ever two lovers completed each other, it was the two of us."

He seemed to leave the story, and it was about to catch some breeze and be swept away, leaving its beautiful notions behind, but I was not satisfied. If this was such a wonderful relationship, what was he doing here with me? A small-minded feeling of jealousy sprang up.

"So… What happened to the two of you?"

He was silent for minute, then said, "Nothing has changed between the two of us, Miss. But my lover was raped and murdered."

As soon as he said that, I felt stricken, and started crying, and something of the feeling in the song this man had just sung came up inside of me. I looked at him, and I saw my own sadness mirrored in his eyes, except in a more profound way. And the way he looked at me, I felt for just a second that he really had meant me.

That night, I was sleeping in a B&B that was in Killarney, and I suddenly felt something touching my arm. I woke up, and Lucas was bending down next to my bed. He put his finger to his lips to tell me not to talk, then motioned for me to follow him. I put on my day clothes and went outside. Our B&B was not far from Killarney Forest, so we walked there, and found ourselves inside. Everything was quiet, except for the night breeze, which spoke like a child's whisper – a little louder than a regular whisper, but with no self-consciousness. The moon was above, and the stars were everywhere. It gave the trees and lakes an eerie, ethereal glow.

"Why are we here?" I found myself whispering, even though no one else was around.

He turned to look at me, and his eyes once again had transformed. This time, the blue had become deep, like the darkness of the depths of the lakes.

"Miss, these parts are just as beautiful during the night as they are during the day, perhaps even more so." His voice put me under a spell, and I followed him into the forest.

The whispering of the breezes seemed to begin speaking. But the language was not English.

"Lucas," I whispered, "I know this is going to make me sound half insane, but I think the breezes in these trees are talking."

"Miss, there is no craziness at night, only a clarity of what we shut our eyes to during the day."

"So… Someone is speaking?" We kept walking, very slowly, and my companion would not answer me.

"It doesn't seem like English," I said.

"At this time of the night, the creatures don't speak the language of invaders, Miss. It's an ancient language."

I felt I could barely breathe, trying to focus on the light of the moon, and trying not to be enveloped by the darkness. The moonlight shimmered on the leaves of the trees above us, and spilled down upon our bodies. Their trunks stood like dark sentinels, and I felt intimidated. I heard a rustle in some bushes nearby, then I saw something sprint away.

"What was THAT?! I still whispered, but more loudly." Lucas wouldn't answer, so I found myself answering… "Was it an animal? It didn't seem like it. It seemed to be running on two feet. What animal around here runs on two feet?" I found myself holding on to the arm of my companion, I didn't want to lose him in the darkness.

"Ireland is not just a place for 4-footed creatures," Lucas said, and continued to walk. "Come, I want you to see something."

We came to a clearing where one of the lakes rippled in the breeze, whispering just like the rest of the forest. I could feel Lucas just barely touching my back, and it sent tingles up my spine. Everything about this stranger – his eyes, his voice, his touch, continued to reach inside of me. I watched the stars' reflection moving around on the darkness of the lake in the soft breezes that brushed its surface. After a few minutes, however, it seemed like the points of light from the sky above were dancing, and then they moved above the waters for just an instant, and I caught my breath…. After that brief moment, they all returned to the water, but then seemed to submerge themselves underneath the lake and disappear.

"Lucas, Lucas…" I whispered, almost breathless. "Did you just see that?"

"See what, Miss?" he chuckled. "In Ireland, you see what you are supposed to see."

The next thing I knew, my eyes were opening up to morning, and the light of dawn was filtering through the curtains of the bedroom windows. I got up, showered and dressed, and went to eat breakfast. Lucas was already waiting for me at the table.

"How did you sleep, Miss?" he said, smiling his good morning at me.

"How did I sleep?" I said, confused. "Well... I am not sure whether I slept. I mean..." Now I was very confused. "Didn't we go somewhere last night?"

The stranger looked at me, and his eyes were a clear bright blue again, the twinkle in them contagious in their mirth. "Ay, I'm sure we did." And that's all he said about it.

Lucas waited for me to eat my breakfast with the host, then we went to the car.

"So, is there somewhere I can take you?" I asked, thinking that he finally needed to get somewhere.

"Actually, I was thinking of taking you somewhere."

"Me? I had planned to drive to the southeast part of Ireland."

"Yes, that's a wonderful plan, but I think there is somewhere else you should see first, a part of Ireland you don't want to miss. We have some beautiful peninsulas in the southwest that give you a view of the sea that you're not going to know by driving east."

"Well, ok." I took out my map, unfolded it, and tried to figure out where I needed to drive to. Lucas came up to me and softly took one of my hands and with the other took away the map.

"Road maps of Ireland are not always good at getting you to where you need to go. Give me your car keys and I'll drive us."

I stood there, debating a bit. I liked having control of driving my car, and yielding it to this stranger seemed too unpredictable. I had only known him for one day, and already I was going to let him drive me somewhere off the map? But his eyes and serious expression were no match for my inner doubt, and I gave him the keys. He took the keys and opened the passenger door for me, then gently patted me on my back.

"Ok, in you get."

I breathed a little deeply to calm myself, and as we drove away, I crossed my fingers inside my mind.

## Chapter 3: Jumping Off a Precipice

I felt strange sitting next to this man who, just 2 days ago, had not been in my life. I watched him as he drove smoothly and confidently along the road, and occasionally he would look toward me and laugh – probably at my obvious nervousness and bewilderment – and ask me, "Are you ok, Miss?" Upon my rather hesitant assurances, he would pat me on the leg in a genial way, and say, "Ease your mind, we are almost there, and you will love it."

New experiences are always a little discomforting. I had planned my trip out, had formed a general plan of which places I would like to see. I had not formed a detailed itinerary, and except for the first night I had not reserved any specific Bed and Breakfasts, but I still had a certain idea of how I had wanted to see Ireland, and now this man, unknown to myself, had disengaged me from my plan. I was trying to process this, and put myself into this new path that we were taking, out on the jutting peninsula.

It wasn't long before we were driving on roads where, just beyond, sat cliffs that fell away into the sea. I looked out my window (for they were on the left), and my mind drifted into the forever-after that the horizon beyond seemed to represent. I could drift on those seas for a lifetime, and I would never find a home, and at some point, in all that drifting, the sea itself would be my home… These are the types of ponderings that took over my brain as I sat next to this stranger who seemed to be driving me into some luxurious oblivion. This is why, when we stopped and were parked at a small place to eat, I was looking around as if I was still bound with some kind of spell. I must have had some kind of dazed look on my face as I turned toward Lucas, because his eyes went into a smile and he lightly tapped my cheek with his hand.

"Come out of it, Miss," he – also lightly – said. "You're going to eat first before we go out for a walk this afternoon along the sea."

And so it was, off my plan, away from my original expectations, I found myself walking next to a handsome Irish man, this perfect stranger, with the grasses bending beneath our steps, toward a precipice and the open sea. Nature seems to have conspired with my visit to give me the most beautiful weather to see Ireland in its most attractive clothing, because the sky rolled blue into the distance, like a marriage with the blue of the sea, and the breeze was just cool enough to stave off the warmth of the August sun. The subtle sound of grass giving way underneath our steps played a soothing song that complemented the silent presence of this stranger.

Finally, we arrived along the cliffs and stopped. I looked over the edge, and the water, far below, ravaged the base every few seconds with an insistent push forward and, crashing against the wall, gave in, only to try again. The sea insisted, bravely fought, lost, then came back again. I felt myself being pulled into its rhythm. Then somewhere in this poetry of the resting and crashing passion of the sea, Lucas's voice drifted into the space between us.

"That's the spirit of this land, Miss."

I could hear his voice reverberate with the waters far below, and I looked over at him, and saw his eyes, that softer afternoon blue, staring out into the distance. His words were seeping into the crevices of my understanding, not only from their meaning, but in the feeling with which they had been said. The wind from the sea, stronger than the breezes we had known in Killarney, caressed his hair, and the sunlight came in afterward and turned the honey brown of his locks into glints of dark gold. In a moment of covetousness, I found myself reaching up and touching his hair. He didn't turn around or make me stop, but the momentary touch was enough to make me want more; I could feel the soft waves…and I was drawn

33

in. I spent a minute running my fingers through his hair, and he stood there in silent acceptance of my touch, like waters receiving a submerged body. Finally, my hand receded to my side.

Then he turned to me and spoke. "It's been a long time since I felt that, Miss."

We continued walking along the cliff. At first, the cliff had seemed a dangerous height, but then I found myself enamored of the majestic sight of the cliffs with the sea joining the sands and rugged wall that came to meet it. I sighed.

"What's on your mind, Miss," said Lucas, breaking the silence.

"I was thinking of my grandma again."

"How so this time? Is this walk reminding you of her?"

"No… It's the sea. We both grew up in a rather land-locked state toward the middle of America, and I think my grandma was the type of person who had wished to see more of the world. She would talk about how one time she went to the East Coast and visited Chincoteague, an island off the coast of Virginia. Just from the way she talked about it… I didn't get a lot of details, but it was the way she talked about going there, that I realized she wished she could have gone farther."

"And how far was that?"

"Beyond that was the open sea, so I suppose she just wanted to keep going that way."

"Ah, you mean come here."

"Yes," I said, laughing a little, "The way she talked and sang songs about Ireland, it was obvious that she wanted to come here, but she never did."

He stopped me in our walk by putting his hand on my arm and looking at me.

"She never did?"

"No. Never." And my sadness increased, I felt a regret for my grandma, and I almost wanted to cry. I must have cried, because Lucas grew even more quiet and intense.

"Miss," he said low and softly, "Are you sure she never came to Ireland?"

"My goodness," I said, through my sadness, "I have said to you 3 times now, she didn't get here. I know my own grandma."

Lucas looked at me, and for some moments the only thing between us was the sound of waves crashing against the cliffs.

"Ok, Miss, if you say so," he said, with even more levity. "But I wonder then how she came to talk about it and feel it so much."

I looked into his eyes, eyes as blue as the afternoon sea, and I tried with all the stubbornness of my practical soul to resist their expression, but the soul inside them came toward me so powerfully, that all I could do was stand there, as still as the ages, and let their wisdom wash over me and my old sensibilities began to erode away.

That night, because we had gotten so far off the beaten path, we could find no Bed and Breakfast. I wasn't sure what to do, and was ready to just sleep in the car, but then my companion, who knew more about Ireland than I did, told me about the law that allows travelers to sleep on the land in any given place for 1 night.

"This is a rule for traditional Irish storytellers who travel and rarely stay in one place, but this benefits gypsies, as well… And it seems like the two of us are gypsies these days."

We found a farmhouse not too far from the cliffs, and Lucas, with some confidence in the traditional hospitality of the Irish, went up to the house to talk to the people who owned the farm. I could see the warm light emanating from the inside of the home, and it was with a positive hope for sleeping somewhere inside that I watched Lucas walking back to me.

"Ok, I arranged for us to sleep inside their barn."

"Their barn? Not inside the home?"

Lucas smiled at me in the evening light. "Miss, the weather is not so cold, and barns are warm in the night. They said they would give us some blankets, and we can make ourselves comfortable. After that, they'll give you an Irish breakfast."

I looked toward the barn, then back to the house. I remembered how my grandmother had talked about sleeping in the barn on her farm sometimes while growing up. I realized how spoiled I had been – I had always slept in a bed in a bedroom. I remembered her telling me how, during the wintertime, the home did not have heat, so her mother would bundle her with blankets, then heat some bricks and put them near her feet. I had never suffered any kind of cold in my sleeping life. What made me better than her?

"Ok, that sounds good," I said to him. And I meant it.

As we lay down for the night next to each other, I smelled the fresh hay as the wind blew through crevices of doors and windows in the barn and blew all of its scents around me. The ground beneath me was softened by some hay that the farmer had allowed us to spread for our bed – I was amazed by this hospitality to strangers. Lucas was next to me, and he could probably sense my unease, so he took my hand and held it as much to say, "Don't worry, nothing will take you away in the night." Even as he slept, his hand continued to hold mine. After an hour of lying there, hearing every small sound of the night inside in the barn, I finally let my worry go to the wind, and drifted off to sleep.

I did not even know what time it was when I could feel the slight tug at my hand. I woke, and saw Lucas getting up, pulling my hand as a gesture to follow him.

"Take your shoes and socks off, Miss," was all he said before we left the barn.

"What? Why?"

"Just trust me on this one."

We left the barn, walking in our bare feet across the fields, and I could feel the rough coolness of the meadow grass beneath my feet. My companion continued to hold my hand, but walked slowly so that I would not trip on anything, and we made our way toward the cliffs of the sea. When we had gotten to the precipice, he sat down, and smoothed the place out next to him. I sat down there with my legs dangling over the edge, and he put his arm around my waist. I think, because we were so close to the precipice, he was worried about my being too tired and losing my balance. I felt awake, but everything seemed dreamlike; the moonlight shown on the sea, making the depths seem even darker for the light on the surface. Although the sky was lit up by millions of stars, the darkness around us was immense. If Lucas had not been so close to me, I may have lost him on the way to the cliff. Coming closer to the cliff with the moon reflecting off the sea, I could see his profile glowing in the moonlight.

"I think this is better at night, Miss. It's just the sea…and you."

"Yes… I wonder…"

"What are you wondering?"

"In the songs my grandma sometimes sang, the story would go something along the lines of a lover waiting for her man to return from the sea."

"Ay."

After a few seconds of gazing, he resumed.

"Many a man lost their soul in the waters. Many an Irish man was a seafaring sort, they lived on the Irish shores and lived off of the sea, but sometimes they died from her, too."

"Her?"

"Ha ha… Of course the sea is a "she"… Many a woman has been the death of men." Then he laughed, and I felt as if he had been joking. Then he became serious. "And many a man was the death of women as well," he added, staring into some unfathomable distance in time.

"Anyway, the sea is a strong lure," he whispered into my ear, and he kissed its skin, still holding me close. And as he kissed the flesh of my ear, a low, mournful song seemed to come from him, and, entering through my ear, swirled inside my head and deep down inside my limbs. The crash of the waves seemed to keep tempo with my breathing as I felt his song going deeper inside of me.

I suddenly felt an overwhelming pressure where I almost couldn't think, and removing myself from Lucas and his arm, I lay down on the grass. I saw all the stars above, and it seemed, in the dense darkness and quiet of the world, I could see and feel the movement of the galaxy. I stretched my arms out into the abyss over the cliff. Lucas was looking down at me for a while, then he took my hand and said,

"Come on."

"Where are we going?"

"Into the water."

I came crashing back into reality and almost crumpled under my shock at this suggestion. "Umm… Mr…. Well… Lucas… I don't think so."

"It's completely ok. I'll hold you on the way down."

I looked over the dark precipice, now more dangerous than beautiful compared to how it had looked in the afternoon sunlight. I heard waves crashing below, and imagined rocks upon which I would be dashed to pieces. Many a damsel had used this method as a way of suicide in old times.

"I know what you're thinking, Miss, and I brought us to a place where you won't feel the danger of shallow waters or rocks."

"I'm sure there are many more things that I haven't imagined which could take my life away."

"I'm sure there are, Miss. Your life could end by crossing the street at the wrong time in your hometown, or by a simple tumble down your home stairs. Is that the glorious way you want to live your life?"

I remained stubborn. I looked into his eyes, which were, like the night before, a dark blue, like the ocean, like the night sky. I lost myself in their depths, and had to pull myself out before I drowned.

"Miss… So many of us go to a precipice and look over its edge, then hang back. We look out at the mystery of the sea beyond, then we turn around and walk back to the comfort of everything that was familiar. Is this the dream your grandma had?"

I caught my breath for a second, thinking of my grandma's life… How she had spent her final years confined to a wheelchair, confined to her regrets, then confined to a small room in a nursing home. I looked out at the sea.

"Let's go," I whispered, and took his hand. He walked back a few steps, taking me with him.

"No, you'll be taking more than that. Wrap your arms around my neck."

When I had done that, he wrapped his arms tightly around my back.

"Don't worry," was all he said, as he grabbed me up off the ground, and ran over the cliff. All I could feel was the tight grip of his arms and the wind rushing against us for those terrifying moments. I closed my eyes, just wanting to feel these last few seconds of my life.

Then I felt the slice of ice-cold water hit my body as I was released, and as my eyes opened the last thing I saw was Lucas going under as I was completely submerged in the raging waters. My survival skills took over, as I felt the rush of the cold water and the push of the waves trying to drag me out to sea; I climbed up to the surface, where I could see the moonlight above, and came into the open night air, choking for breath, feeling reborn.

Lucas took my hand and looked at me with a strong expression in his eyes. He seemed to pause for a moment, considering something, then seemed to change his mind.

"Come on, Miss, you can't linger in these waters, they will take you for their bride if you hesitate too long."

We both swam toward a little area down the way that had a place to stand on the ground, and we got out of the water.

I looked up at the wall of cliffs surrounding us.

"Lucas, how are we supposed to get back?"

"Miss, once you have jumped over the edge of the precipice, there is no going back."

He started to take off his shirt and pants, and I was shocked for the second time that night.

"What are you doing?"

"Miss, I'm just stripping my clothes off because I like the feel of the surf and night air directly on my skin." He looked at me for a minute, shivering in my wet clothes. "You need to do the same yourself. It will make you stronger. And it will bring you back to yourself."

I had no idea what he meant by that, but I looked at him and shook my head, holding my clothes tightly to myself. "Not on your life. Jumping over one cliff tonight was enough for me."

Lucas laughed, and said, "Suit yourself. You Americans are so conscious about your skin. I'll never understand it. Out of consideration for your sensitivity, I'll go over here." And he went a few steps away, then stripped the last piece of clothing off his body. As he stood there, the spray of the surf washing over his body, his clothes drying in the wind from the waves, I kept dripping and shivering, fully clothed. Nevertheless, I watched him. It would have been impossible not to – the open space was not very big, and the moonlight shone on his skin with a hauntingly white iridescence. His legs were muscular, and his chest was bare, except for the honey-brown hair near the top, and then the soft, yet firm skin of his arms… Well, I had already experienced their strength. He looked strong without being brawny, which lent a beautiful vulnerability to his body. His skin shone in the night with a purity and emanated strength and assurance through his movements. There was no shyness, but he wasn't showing anything off, either. I didn't need to look at the sea or the surf anymore – I felt like I was seeing it in him. And I suddenly realized that I wasn't feeling very cold anymore, despite the winds and my wet body.

My eyes opened as I felt like I was being gently nudged.

"It's morning, Miss," Lucas said to me with a smile.

I looked around and saw the familiar barn. But my clothes felt a little damp.

"Lucas… Where…. Did we go somewhere last night?"

He chuckled. "Only you know that, Miss."

After I ate breakfast, Lucas looked at me. "Where do you want to go?"

"Shouldn't I be asking you that?" I said, then realized he was going wherever I was. "I would love to see some of those sheep farms in Ireland. I've been in Ireland for a few days now, and I haven't run into a single sheep."

Lucas's eyes crinkled into an Irish smile, and he said, "Ok, we'll be finding some sheep today, then." Before he got into the driver's seat, he rested his arms on the car frame, bent down, and looked at me sitting in the passenger seat.

"You're really easy to please, Miss."

## Chapter 4: The Kiss of Pure Waters

We had left the lonely peninsula behind us, and were back on the highway for a while. I looked at the landscape and realized something about Ireland that was so different from my own country's landscape. When I traveled on highways in the U.S., I was accustomed to seeing all the billboards on the side of the roads, advertising something or another. Usually, as I passed towns, there were always boards and signs reminding me of all the fast food and restaurant chains that were in those towns. What suddenly struck me was that, in my few days in Ireland, I had not experienced any "chain" stores. It was a strange realization, that perhaps a people could exist without blanket uniformity of businesses.

My companion must have felt something, because he glanced at me, and said, "What's on your mind, Miss. You're quieter than usual."

I didn't really want to talk about the fact that I had not seen any McDonalds or Starbucks.

"I just think it's strange…." And for a lack of a topic… "I haven't seen any chain stores in Ireland yet, like McDonalds or Starbucks."

"Oh my days, would you be wanting to see these stores?" And he laughed.

"Well, to be honest… No. I was just thinking how I've gotten used to seeing chain stores like that everywhere I go that I would consider "civilization", and not seeing them and realizing I have been able to live without them, and… well, perhaps live better without them…"

"Ay, it makes me sad when people get used to seeing things that are always the same, and then need that to feel comfortable. But I don't know how you define civilization, Miss. There's always something that's inside of us…" He stopped for a bit. "Something is always inside of us, Miss. Civilization, to me, is a word for people who like to pour concrete over everything."

"Yeah. That makes me remember a conversation I had with my grandma. We were walking in a neighborhood near where she lived, and she wanted to show me a forest, because she knew I loved forests, and she wanted to show me a place in the area that still had a small forest with beautiful trees. But when we got there, she stopped and seemed confused. She kept looking at the place, and said, 'I don't know what happened. Where is the forest?' As we stood there, looking at the neighborhood that had been built up where the forest supposedly used to be, I could feel her growing frustration."

"Supposedly? Why do you say that, Miss?"

As he was saying that, he turned off from the highway and onto a much narrower road. We began to drive into the hilly countryside. Everything became greener around us.

"Well, I had no proof that there had been a forest there. It was just a neighborhood of houses."

"You had her memory. That was proof enough."

"I guess," I said, not totally convinced. "It seemed that for years afterward, I mean, *for years*, she would bring that up, how disappointed she was that they had torn down that forest to build up more houses. I don't know if she kept saying that to convince herself that her memory of the forest was real, or perhaps it was something deeper."

"What's that?"

"I think she wanted to return to something more real and pure. In her younger days, she had loved being in the city, but as she got older it seemed like she wanted to go back to the way things had been as she was growing up. She grew up in the countryside, surrounded by trees, and maybe, as her life slowed down, she found that the pace of society was speeding up and going too fast. I think when she was young she liked diversion, which the city held for her, but the changes went beyond her, and she just wanted to go back."

"You seem to have thought a lot about her."

"Always."

After a few minutes, Lucas switched off the radio with an impatient gesture. "Enough of that music." Then he turned to me again, while trying to navigate the country roads, "So, your grandma liked singing Irish songs. What song did she love the most?"

"The one I remember her singing a lot was "When Irish Eyes Are Smiling."

"Oh, it be this one? Yes, that's a pretty tune."

Within the next minute, as the sun shone on the hills and the fresh air blew in our faces from the open car windows, Lucas started to hum the song. I began to smile in spite of myself, and started humming along. Then he began to softly sing the lyrics, and I stopped and just listened to him, feeling everything within myself being pulled asunder. I had never been so affected by a voice before.

Lucas pulled the car over to the left on the narrow road and put on the brake, and looked at me. I wouldn't look at him. Instead, I looked to the left outside my window. He reached over under my chin and, putting his hand on my left cheek, moved my face toward him. I just looked down.

"Look at me, Miss."

I looked into those eyes whose depths seemed to change according to my own emotion, and right now they were the blue of past skies.

"We're singing about smiling Irish eyes, and you are so sad all the time. Where are you?"

I couldn't tell him what his voice had just done to me, how it had touched something, some kind of memory and pulled it up with all of its force, and made me feel things all over again that I thought had been lost, or that in some ways I had wanted to lose. It had been so much easier not to feel.

"I'm not Irish," I told him.

"How are you thinking that?" He kept his hand on my cheek, and I could only feel the skin of his fingers.

"I don't know," I said, trying to clear my head. "I guess it's because my grandma is only part of my ancestry. I'm 50% Italian, and then some parts of other nationalities, I don't have those smiling Irish eyes."

He laughed, and his own eyes filled with that laughter, and the back of his hand spread across the side of my face as he wiped away some of my tears.

"Italian? Oh, those Italians. They love to eat a lot of food and drink a lot of wine, then after they use up all their happiness on the meal they get angry and passionate until the next time they get to eat." Then he grew quiet. "Miss, the Irish are a bit different. We have a deep memory, a memory for things that many times have been gone so long that no one would believe they had been there. Our laughter and smiles run deep, as well, but it's because they need to be the antidote to the sorrow we feel."

After he had wiped away the tears on my left cheek, his hand moved over and wiped the tears still left on the right side of my face. Then he ran his fingers through some of my hair, and very subtly nodded.

"Don't fret, Miss. You're Irish."

Then he pointed toward the front of the car.

"And here come some of your sheep right now."

As he put the car back in drive, Lucas had to go very slowly and navigate around some sheep who had meandered onto the already narrow road.

We drove for just a short while on these country roads, until we found a sheep farm in the hills that had a sign saying it served lunch. Since we both had been driving for a while with only digestive biscuits for me to eat, we stopped here for lunch. The lunch was very simple, just a sandwich. We decided to talk to the owner who was running the place.

"Hi, Missus," Lucas said, "Do you think we could take a stroll around your grounds for a while? We've got a tourist from the States who would love to see a sheep farm."

I blushed, and said, "Yeah, well, where I come from it's mainly just cornfields. I would love to see the sheep herds here."

The host laughed a bit, "Well, you're easy to please." Then added, "Will you be needing some water?"

"Yes, ma'am," my companion said.

"Well, if you have some empty water bottles, I'll give you water from my own farm. My house pumps up pure water from the stream. I think you'll really enjoy it."

Before I could protest, Lucas said, "That sounds wonderful, ma'am. I'll get some bottles from our car and you can fill them up as you please."

I watched as the woman turned the water on in the sink and filled our bottles up, and I thought for sure that Lucas must have been a crazy man that was trying to ruin my vacation. I had remembered my vacation to Bogota, Colombia, where I had had the misfortune to go out to a farm with my friend and drink unpasteurized cow's milk. All the others had had it before, so it was nothing for them; for me, however, it took its revenge on the rest of my week, and the remaining days had been more of an exercise in how not to be miserable. Being here in Ireland, where a while could be spent driving out in the middle with nowhere to go... where would I go?

Lucas extended his arm to me, bottle in hand, urging me to take it with that beautiful Irish smile on his face. Ok, I would take it, but I would not drink it. He would have to do more than smile to make me drink it, I thought to myself.

Lucas laughed. "I can see the expression on your face, Miss. Don't worry. You'll love it." He opened the door for me then put his hand around my waist as he guided me toward the hills.

"The sheep are herding this way. Come on, we can watch them."

We made our way into the hills and walked among the long grasses. I did as best as I could to keep up with my companion, and when he saw that I was struggling to get up the incline, he would go a bit slower, so we were walking together. There were parts that were somewhat slippery to navigate, and he seemed to know it, so he would hold his hand to my arm and I would accept it. The farmhouse and café had long fallen out of view; we were just in the hills now, and I could see the sheep. As we stood there, I looked out over the rolling countryside and hills, and the sheep moving among them, unworried and, well… seemingly blissful. I felt calmer than I had in years. I looked up at Lucas, who had been looking at me.

"Ah, Miss, there's a smile."

"Can we just sit here for a while?"

"Of course, if you don't worry about getting your arse a bit wet, Miss. The dews linger a little bit longer in these hills than in other places, and the grass may still be a bit damp."

I snickered. "Ok, so it's going to look like I wet my pants." Then I looked out at the sheep. "I don't think they will judge me for it."

"That's the spirit, Miss."

We sat next to each other, and I gazed out at the sheep. I think I could have watched this pastoral paradise the rest of the day, just because I knew that when I went back to my homeland I would never get to see this.

"Why are there different colored markings on the sheep, Lucas?"

"Oh, that's so the farmers can identify which sheep belongs to them. But they can come out here and mingle, and enjoy their grasses."

"And enjoy their lives," I sighed.

"Ay."

As we continued to gaze, Lucas suddenly said, "I really like you, Miss."

I was shocked. "You LIKE me?" Then I laughed away my unease and embarrassment. "What inspired this outburst?"

He kind of bent his head from side to side, as if he was considering the vantage point in the distance, and finding the answer there. Then he leaned toward me and looked a bit my way, but not completely at my face.

"I like you because, with you, I feel like I'm with my equal."

What he had said didn't seem romantic on the surface, but nevertheless it made me blush. He stopped speaking as if it was something already understood between us, but I wanted to hear more. This is not something I had ever heard from a man in my life. Usually, in my experience, men preferred to dominate women, or condescend to them, or objectify them, dismissing the existence of intelligence. And now here was a man – an attractive man – extolling my virtue of equality with himself. Who was this apparition?

"If you don't mind… Can you explain what you mean?"

"Ah, so you don't feel this?"

"Lucas…. It's not about feeling. It's about the experience. I have never experienced this in my country with a male, this declaration of…equality."

He didn't laugh at this, but merely explained. "Miss, I feel comfortable with you, and I don't feel judged in any critical way. I feel as if we have just been moving together throughout this space, sharing time together. It hasn't been a struggle or a competition." He sighed. "It seems like most women fall on two ends of a spectrum, and rarely achieve that balance in the middle. There is the woman who clings on a man and is always needing his support for her life because she can't think of anything for herself. She is always walking behind the man, and putting him above her, expecting him to be her superman, never daring to take any challenges herself. Those types of women… Well, the men take care of them, but they leave us exhausted." He paused again. "Then there is the other type of woman, who is always trying to walk ahead of the man, setting out to prove that she is just as good or better than he is, and overcompensates in the relationship. The man is left feeling that he is always having to run to keep up with this woman, never being able to walk in a natural way. This type of woman becomes so self-sufficient that it seems like there is nothing left for the man but to be some kind of entertainer to make her laugh, and beyond that we are useless. Men do not want to have to always be a superman, but we want to feel as if we have some kind of strength that is part of the relationship."

"So, I like you, Miss. You have got yourself, but you want me there, too – we can be right by each other's side."

"Lucas, I'm going to be honest with you…. I think you are being a bit unfair to women."

"How is that, Miss?" He dusted some grass that had blown onto his jeans, then looked at me with interest in his afternoon-blue eyes. I looked back at them, finding my way deep inside.

"Because… The way a woman falls on that spectrum says less about how she is as a woman and more about how she feels about the man. If she finds a man that is a perfect fit for her soul, she is not going to be running ahead or lagging behind – she's going to be right at his side. So, the problem is not women necessarily, but that these women are not waiting to find that person that fits their soul."

Lucas continued to gaze at me.

"You know another thing I like about you, Miss."

"What's that?"

"I've been in Ireland all these years of my existence, and I have experienced a lot of her. But when I go around with you and see how you look at everything…" He put the fingers of his right hand up to the side of my face next to my right eye… "It's like I can see her for the first time all over again. And just in your reactions, in your eyes, I am discovering something new."

Without even thinking about what I was saying, I cleared my dry throat and said, "I think I need some water."

"Oh yes, we need to drink some of this water."

To my dismay, Lucas produced the two bottles of water that the woman had poured for us earlier. I shook my head. He looked at me and shook his head, but in a laughing disbelief.

"You can't refuse this water. You'll never get anything this pure and sweet anywhere else, I can tell you now."

There was a memory in my mind of Colombia and drinking coffee, and realizing that the richness of the coffee had to do with the water. I had brought the same coffee home and made it at home, but it didn't taste the same. But there was a difference between drinking water that had been boiled and water that had just been pumped up from some farmland stream.

"I'm sure I won't. But I can't chance the effects."

Lucas looked at me with some disappointment. "You still haven't learned to have some faith? Not willing to take a chance on something different?"

I thought about what had happened – if it had indeed happened – the night before, but couldn't even confirm if I had indeed done what I thought I had done. But this was the light of day, truly reality, and I would really be taking this drink. I shook my head.

"Ok, Miss, I think we need to work out some kind of compromise. How about if I give you an amount that will be so small that it will have no effect on you?"

"How will you do that?"

He took the bottle and gently tipped it until a few drops landed on his fingers.

"Here, Miss. You have to taste this." He extended his fingers toward my lips. As he did so, he looked at me with such a sincerity that the blue of the afternoon sky in his eyes became all-encompassing. I just nodded my head slightly, and he brought his fingers up to my lips. I touched my lips to his fingers and just barely touched my tongue to their skin. I felt like I was receiving some kind of Communion, and my body seemed to be outside of itself. There was not enough water to swallow, just enough to taste, and the water had a sweetness that I had never tasted in water before. It stayed on my tongue; and Lucas softly stroked my lips with his fingers, wetting them with the residual moisture.

That night I was awakened again, and this time Lucas and I found that stream. Just like the night before, we had gone barefoot, and now he told me,

"This is not the ocean, but they are refreshing waters. Get in and let's have a walk."

I tested the water with my foot, and it was cool, but refreshingly cool, not cold like the ocean. I felt my entire body sinking into its comfortable feel, even though it only went about 8 inches up my legs at its deepest point. Lucas got inside after me, and we walked upstream. The stream was in an area surrounded by trees, and the darkness was much more profound than the night before. The heights of the trees filtered out most of the starlight, so it was hard to see where I was going. Lucas walked close behind me, holding me at my hips. He seemed to know this stream intimately; he knew intuitively where each place in the stream was where I could have tripped or lost my balance, and he protectively gripped my sides right before we came to that point. I would just slightly slide over a stone, then regain my balance, and Lucas would relax his grip. Between the warmth of his body behind me and the refreshing cool current that bubbled quietly in the darkness, I felt as if I was moving forward through some kind of spell. Then I felt Lucas lean near to my ear and whisper,

"Just a little further, Miss." His breath tickled my skin and I could feel myself moving closer to something, yet I had no clear understanding of the destination.

Then we came to a little clearing in the stream. I had no idea how far we had walked; it didn't seem like it should have been, but it felt like we had walked a long distance into this forest and for an indefinable amount of time. Every night I spent with this man, I lost my sense of the minutes and the hours.

Lucas put his arms around my waist to stop me, then moved his face near my cheek. I could feel the combination of smooth and rough skin. "Look forward a ways, Miss. There it is."

I peered into the darkness and could hear something pouring out. Then I saw glints of light, and finally made out water pouring out of an opening in the ground, the water falling and feeding the stream where we were standing.

"Come on, Miss. Let's take a drink."

We both walked over to the little fountain, and he turned to me.

"You've some more courage now, Miss. You go first."

I was scared of the darkness and this water that seemed to emerge out of nowhere, coming from the depths of the earth, but I felt pulled toward it, and put my hands under the water. It splashed gently in my cupped palms, and some of it splashed out, but I bent down and took a long drink. The water was the purest I had tasted, and was as sweet as the fruits of the world. The sweetness was subtle, but it ran down my tongue and throat like liquid honey. I wanted to take another drink, but something told me that one draught was enough. I bent down and cupped my hands again, and filled them with water. I turned around to my companion. His honey brown hair lay like beautiful dark waves, and his body was a silhouette in the darkness. The little light that filtered down from the night sky through the forest was mirrored in the depths of his eyes and the soft white skin of his face; for a second he seemed to transcend the man I had known during the day. I held my hands toward him, offering him a drink.

"Your turn," I said.

"Hey, Miss... Are you enticing me into some sin?"

"No… No… This offering is like redemption," I said, smiling.

He came to me and cupped my hands in his, then bent down and drank. Then he separated my hands; as the remaining drops fell into the pool of water beneath us, he moved my hands toward him, and I cupped his face in my palms.

"Miss, Miss," I heard a familiar voice say, and I slowly opened my eyes. "You seem to like oversleeping. You missed breakfast."

I looked around at the room of the B&B where I was staying, trying to regain my sense of place.

"Did I?" I said to him. "It's strange, but I don't feel hungry."

"Well, in that case, up with yourself. Get dressed because I'm sure our host is going to charge you a fee for being lazy if you don't get yourself around soon." I looked at him, and knew by the laughter in his eyes that he was joking. Nevertheless, I got up and got my stuff around.

"I think I would like to go to the south part of Ireland," I told him.

"Yes, we can go there. There are some lovely towns along the coast."

It was at this point that I realized I wanted him to continue traveling with me. I guess my mind was a little slow, finally catching up with my feeling.

## Chapter 5: A Return to Childhood

We drove to a town near the southern tip of Ireland, and I finally experienced some town-centered tourist destinations. We found an old prison and I wanted to do a tour of this, just to see the culture of imprisonment. I wasn't quite sure what attracted to me to this particular place, but we went there and walked through the dingy halls and cells, reading the stories of people who had been incarcerated there, and why, and what kind of life they led in these cells. I thought it was a bit ironic, contemplating the modern state of prisons in America... Certainly, prisons were not like homes (and why should they be, they are for people who had committed a crime), but the conditions were much better than these, and prisoners were fed, given medical care... I tried not to think too politically, then Lucas suddenly sighed.

"What's wrong?" I asked.

"Prisons always make me a little sad, Miss. They are a mark of that civilization man; when he pours concrete, he also makes his rules, and then takes away the freedom of those who don't like those rules."

I stood there, looking at Lucas's beautiful profile, which was tinged with sadness for the first time since I had met him. But I couldn't agree with his idea.

"Would you rather have society devolve into chaos, where people do anything they want?"

"Oh, Miss, you don't have much faith in the human spirit. Look at the wilderness parts of the world, the few that are still left. There is a natural order to those things. Animals don't just go around killing for their jollies, they kill to eat, and the animals that would otherwise overrun the earth are kept in a balance. When men live in the wilderness, they likewise have a survival spirit. They need to eat, but everything else is kept in its place. They take what they need for where they rest their head, but they don't feel the need to spread their claim out. They kill an animal in the forest, but they don't lay waste to the whole forest."

Lucas turned his head to look toward me.

"And then of course, there may be those who violate the natural order of things. It has been occurring since the first man that came out of his mother's womb. The urge to kill their fellow brothers has always seemed to be something beneath the surface of men's souls."

"Yes, like people killing in the name of their religion, or for their particular god."

"Ay. There is that. And the killing for jealousy and covetousness. There are many reasons why people kill, that only seem to be justified in this hazy place of the human heart, but are not justified in the world beyond. And then the killing of humans for food and survival – that seems like an irrational feat, when you consider how big the world used to be. But in nature, there was always a counter-balance to such violence, she always found a way to bring justice to humans in the end. There were no prisons, just nature's vengeance."

"So nature is also a "she"?"

"Ay, everything that overwhelms the males of the human world is a 'she'." And he looked at me with a little smile playing on his lips.

"And anything you seek to control is also a 'she'," I rejoined.

"Of course. It's bringing things back into balance."

I silently chuckled at this, and felt his strong masculinity emanating from his skin. I wondered where we were at this point. But I kept those feelings to myself.

"But you still didn't explain why you have such a negative feeling toward prisons in cities."

He nodded his head slowly. "Yes, this is true. I haven't. I can't explain it to you fully, but it be strange to me, when you have a poor man who is trying to survive by taking a bit of bread for himself for one day, and the rich man who has a storehouse for years puts him in prison for being a criminal. It goes against the law of nature. I don't even understand how that type of justice even comes from inside a person. Where is their reason?"

I shivered a bit inside of myself as a cold breeze wandered through the jail cells. I took Lucas's hand and pulled him. "Come on, let's go," I said.

"Where are we going?"

"Out of the city."

He didn't protest this, so we left this prison. As we came out of the building, he stopped me and made me turn around, then pointed up. We both looked at the mannequin figure hanging from a rope over the doorway of the prison.

"There's a man," he said.

I laughed. "Come on, Lucas. It's a mannequin made to represent a man."

"That's what they want you to think," he said. He still paused, looking up at the figure. "It's a message," he said quietly.

"I know. They wanted to show how people get punished when they break the law."

"Ah, Miss. You still don't understand everything. It's before your breaking of law. It's a message that they want to choke the life out of you."

Just then, a wind picked up and the mannequin moved. I almost jumped out of my skin.

"Come on, Lucas."

We got in the car, and this time I drove. I drove out of the city, and soon the concrete gave way to the natural landscape of Ireland, and I felt both of us were breathing more freely again. I automatically reached for the radio, but then Lucas's hand stopped me.

"Don't be doing that. You don't need that manufactured music. Certainly there is something inside of you that you can sing." And he gently played with the fingers of my left hand as I used my right hand for the steering wheel.

"Well, it's an American song."

"Let's hear it."

I began to sing the first verse, feeling self-conscious because this man next to me could sing so beautifully, but I kept my voice low enough so that the song was expressive without being intrusive upon the calm feeling inside the car. Lucas turned to the side and leaned on his seat, and I could feel him listening to me and looking at me. My heart beat inside my throat, but I kept singing. I finished the song, and for a minute there was complete silence. My companion was still sitting there, looking at me. Then he finally spoke.

"That's a right nice song, Miss."

I thought he would then sing his own song, since his voice was so softly passionate, and I found myself wanting to hear his voice, but then he said,

"Sing me another."

I could feel my cheeks burning, because this was not what I had expected from a man, and yet it was a perfect outcome. I went through my mental collection of songs, and picked out another that I could sing, and he listened to me again.

After I had finished, he continued to sit there for a while, and I started to realize that perhaps he was daydreaming, he was so quiet. I just briefly turned toward him, and his eyes were as blue as the hills around us were green, and just as rich in meaning. I turned back to watch the road.

"What are you thinking, Lucas?" I asked, curious.

"Just dreaming, Miss." And I could hear his soft breathing next to me, the car was so quiet.

"So where will you be going next, Miss?"

"I'm not sure," I answered truthfully. "I'm just driving South, and when I get there, we'll get out."

"No maps or destinations?" he said softly.

"Not this time," I said.

"That's the spirit," he said, and I could feel him sigh contentedly. I looked at him and saw his eyes gazing back at me, and as I turned back to watch the road, I felt myself going deeper inside a pathway that led into a world of water, earth and sky, with nothing in between. And the steps were accompanied by the soft, rhythmic breath of this stranger beside me.

When we reached a quaint hamlet by the sea, I told Lucas I needed to buy some souvenirs, so we found a shop that was on a hill overlooking the sea. If anything inspired one to feel Ireland while buying knickknacks, it was this store.

As I shopped around the store, Lucas seemed annoyed. I stopped and turned toward him.

"What is wrong with you?" I said.

"I'm a bit confused, Miss. Why are you buying these things? They are just things."

I looked at him in surprise. "Well… Of course I'm buying these things as gifts for my family back home." After I said that, I went to the shelf with crystal-made goods, and was amazed at their beauty. Lucas stood on the other side of the shelf and stared at me through the shelf opening.

"I don't understand what you mean."

I looked up at him, and watched him staring at me as the hanging crystal objects caught little pieces of light and played on the skin of his face. Prisms were dancing deep inside his eyes.

I was confused. "What do you mean, you don't understand what I mean? These souvenirs... It's typical when people travel that they buy gifts to give to people when they go back home."

I tried to go back to looking at the crystal objects, but I looked up and saw my companion leaning on the shelf and intently peering at me, and I could not tear my eyes away from him. The prisms danced around his soft, wavy hair as little breezes from nowhere made the dangling crystal objects move around in the light. I felt hypnotized by his stare, half serious, half confused.

"I don't understand, Miss. Where are you going?"

I felt a little disoriented, because the question was pushing an intent upon me that I didn't understand; this man's spirit was so powerful, that I had to gather my thoughts to express what should have been a simple response.

"Well... I'm going... After I'm done with this travel, I'm going home."

"But where is that?"

"Come on, Lucas. You know where I'm from. It's America."

Lucas looked taken aback, and his facial expression seemed to be filled with sorrow. It was making me a bit distressed and I didn't know why, so I tried to go back to looking at the souvenirs. I picked up a pretty crystal piece and saw my reflection sliced into several different tiny pieces. Suddenly I saw the tiny pieces move – another image was inside the crystal. Then a familiar hand closed over the piece and Lucas's body was close against my back. He gently took the object out of my grasp and whispered into my ear,

"Let it go, Miss. Please let it go."

And for some reason, I only bought one thing – for myself.

After we left the shop, we walked along the short cliff for a pace until we finally came to an area that was level with the sea. The day had turned grey and cloudy, and a bit cool. I had brought my jacket with me from the car, and now I put it on. We took our shoes off and waded into the waters, which were as clear as glass. I could feel the purity in the sea; I had never experienced this before – most of the waters I had swum in were murky or dirty.

"The water is so clear," I said to Lucas, who was walking around looking at the sea bottom swirling around his feet. His shirt, without the sun shining, was a deeper shade of white, and his skin was a bit deeper in hue; his hair blew in swirls around his forehead and face, and as he looked at me I felt for a second that I was looking at an angel. But then he looked up at me – and I was sure of it.

"Yes, Miss. These are untainted waters – see how calm they are."

After we had finished wading through the water, we sat on the shore for a while. I looked inside the bag at the souvenir piece that I had bought. He took it out of the bag, and looked at it. It was a little piece of wood with a pair of baby shoes on them, and some cute Irish expression.

"Why did you buy this?" he said.

"Oh," I said, leaning against his arm, looking at the little artifact of my memory, "That is for me, just a symbol of a memory of my grandma."

Lucas traced the little shoes with his fingers, then said, "How is this bringing your grandmother to you?" He looked toward me.

As I watched his fingers trace the delicate lines of the little shoes, I felt myself going back 26 years in time, to when I was 5 years old.

"It was my grandma…" I started, but then I said, "When I was 5 years old, I still had not learned how to tie my own shoes. I wanted to learn, because I felt being able to tie my own shoes was a step toward independence, I could feel it, even at the age of 5. But my parents were too busy to show me. Perhaps it was the result of being the last child, the result of just getting too busy with life, but being taught how to tie my own shoes, like a lot of the little things in my life, was something that was overlooked and forgotten."

I paused as I assessed my inner reaction.

"I know this is just a ridiculous thing, but all those months of wanting to learn how to tie my shoes and not receiving the attention… It made me feel… Kind of forgotten."

"Kind of forgotten?" Lucas said. What do you mean by 'kind of'?"

"I mean… Well… I guess I mean completely."

"Mm hmm," said Lucas, then he handed the trinket to me and stretched his hands out behind his back and stretched out his legs. He looked out at the sea, and the sea and his eyes mirrored each other, as they became a greyish blue. "So where does your grandmother come into this?"

"Well, my parents and siblings went on a vacation, and I stayed with my grandmother. One of those days, it was late morning or early afternoon, because I remember the living room was already completely bathed in light, she sat in our grandfather's comfortable chair and had me come up into her lap. My grandmother's lap was probably one of the warmest, safest places on earth to my young self; she had a curvy shape with just the right amount of fat to feel warm and soft to my little girl's body, and she wrapped her arms around me. She told me she was going to show me how to tie my shoes."

Lucas didn't say anything, he just glanced at me, then nodded his head, and continued looking at the shore of the sea as the breeze tangled around and played in his hair.

"You can imagine how thrilled I was. So she gave me the instructions, her arms around me, her hands on the shoe laces… She did every step slowly as she explained the process perfectly for a little child… Take these two laces, and make sure they are even, like this; then cross them over each other, then put this one through here like this…" And as I remembered this, I found myself enacting out the lesson… "Then make a loop with the left, and tie the right around the bottom of it, like this… Then put the lace inside like this as a loop, then pull it through, tightening the 2 loops together as you pull them apart… and then they are tied together tight. See?"

And I felt as if I had accomplished my little 5-year old feat all over again, as my hands enacted the magic of the tying together in the air, and I looked at Lucas in innocent triumph, smiling as if I had just learned it for the first time. He looked at me, but he didn't seem to share my joy. He seemed to be a million miles away… Or a million years away. Then suddenly he spoke, and his voice was low and serious.

"It's really wonderful how she did that."

"What? Taught me how to tie my shoes? Of course. Or I might be walking around barefoot for the rest of my life." And with some humor, I looked at my bare feet in the sand.

Suddenly, Lucas swung his legs over and moved behind me, and the next thing I knew he was sitting behind me, leaning against my back, his legs wrapped on either side of me. I could hear his voice in my ear, as soft as the waves in the breeze.

"Tying the shoes was just a process, Miss. The way she held you was the feeling that kept it with you."

After he said that, he wrapped his arms around my waist, and I could feel the gentle masculine pressure of those arms on my stomach. His body felt so warm against mine.

"Miss, can you do me a favor."

"What is that."

"Sing me another song. Another one your grandma sang for you."

I could barely think as some tears fell down my face; my mind was running back into my memory, first heavy like an adult, then faster, the younger I became, and suddenly, I was a child, running helter-skelter around the yard and playground of my youth near my grandma's house, singing my own songs in the sunshine; then the sunshine slowly descended into the night, and my grandma was tucking me in, singing in that aging but sentimental voice of hers, "You are my sunshine, my only sunshine, you make me happy, when skies are grey; you'll never know dear, how much I love you, please don't take my sunshine away."

As I sang, Lucas rested his head on my shoulder, and I felt like I was binding something over time together; I could feel the soft, tickling roughness of his jaw's hair against my neck, and his wavy locks like deep honey on my cheek. I could feel him listening to me sing, so I sang for my grandma, but I also sang for him. As I finished singing the chorus for the second time, he joined me in a subtle whisper, and the song sank into my shoulder and tingled down my arm. There were some moments of silence as we just listened to the gentle lap of the sea overspread with clouds, then still leaning on my shoulder, he said,

"Yes... Please don't, Miss."

That night, we didn't bother putting our day clothes back on; somewhere in the middle of the dark hours, I got up with him and, with my thin bedclothes still clinging to my skin, we walked barefoot along the empty, silent roads. It felt as if everyone had abandoned the town or was in some kind of deep, fairytale-like sleep, there was such darkness and tranquility along the roads as we walked, hand-in-hand. We eventually reached the shores of the beach we had walked in during the day. I looked at the sea, and the gentle waves caught the moonlight, seeming to drink in its power. I looked at Lucas, and his face and the bare parts of his body seemed to also absorb the moonlight. Everything was too quiet; I could hear the man next to me breathing with the rhythm of the sea.

"Where do you think we're going tonight, Miss," he said.

"I already know."

Together, we talked toward the sea, and the water lapped around our ankles. We continued walking, and it reached our thighs. I started to feel the cold of the night sea, but we continued to walk until the water was up to our waists. At that point, Lucas turned to me.

"Miss, lend me your back."

"My back?"

"Come here, lie down on the water."

Even though the water was cold, its motion was nearly still. I lay down on its surface, floating, staring at the moon. Just as I had a

69

few nights earlier, I gazed at the stars, but this time I was cradled in gently moving waters. Then Lucas came up to me and wrapped his arm underneath my back and my knees, and held me up.

"What are we doing?" I asked, confused.

"We're going in."

"What? In where?"

"It's okay, Miss. Just stay in my arms."

Lucas walked deeper into the sea, and it began to immerse my body; I struggled for a brief second, and was scared; he kept walking, and the water kept getting deeper, and at the last moment I held my breath as we went under.

I don't know how long I was under water, I couldn't count time in the darkness that surrounded me. Lucas continued to hold me, and there was a weightlessness and ease in this embrace, until suddenly I felt his arms gripping me more strongly again, and I was coming out into the open air again, out of the water. He was taking me back toward the shore, and the water dripped off of his hair, streaming in little rivulets down his face at first, then the breeze of the night air began to drink up the water from our clothes and skin, and it felt refreshing.

He took me to the sand, and, still holding me, he sat down. I sat in his lap, and he kept his arms around me, slowly removing strands of wet hair from my face. I had no idea where we were, but I felt completely protected, like a little child in a soft blanket. I looked around. It seemed to be the same landscape, but all the buildings and houses of the little hamlet were no longer there; instead, there was only the natural landscape of Ireland. The sky above seemed even darker, and the stars were brighter than before against the blackness. The stars and their shimmering mirror in the sea was the only light on the land, and if I had not been lying against him, I may not have been able to see this man who had become my strange, yet familiar companion. I thought I could hear the sounds of creatures around us. I felt the air was easier to breathe.

"Lucas," I whispered, even though there was no reason to whisper, "Where are we? It seems like where we were, but everything has changed."

"Ay, Miss. Everything has changed. Now it's the way it was."

"But…" I closed my eyes. "But how do we get back to where we were?"

"Miss." Lucas said this one word. My eyes were still closed, trying to process this transformation. He was quiet for so long, I opened my eyes and looked at his face. His eyes were the deepest, darkest blue they had been yet, but deep inside they also seemed to have a burning light. Once he saw me looking at him, he resumed.

"Miss," he sighed. "But we are back to where we were."

All of a sudden, I experienced this strange sensation inside my heart. I felt like I had been waiting ages for him, but this was not possible. I had only been with him for a few days.

"Ah, Miss. Your memory is still not clear."

His face was so close to mine as he cradled my body in his arms, and there was something inside of me that felt I had been here before, but I couldn't remember. Nothing seemed familiar, but something sentimental was being touched inside my senses. He watched me, seeming to wait for something, and I could not understand what it was… A look of recognition?

After waiting a while in the immense darkness, he said,

"Don't worry about it, Miss."

Then he leaned down and his lips just barely touched my lips, and—

I felt some water being sprinkled on my face. I opened my eyes, and the late morning light was already brightening up the room in the inn where Lucas and I had stayed.

"Miss," my companion said apologetically. "I didn't want to do that to you, sprinkle water on you like that, but nothing else seemed to be waking you up."

I looked at him for a moment.

"Then maybe you should have let me sleep."

"Miss, you don't mean that," he said laughingly. "You can't sleep through Ireland like that. Get yourself up, I know you want to start to go back up north on the east side of her today, and I have a lovely place I want you to see."

## Chapter 6: The Light at Dawn

I let Lucas drive this time, because I felt really bewildered that morning. I felt as if I was breathing differently than I had before; I could breathe more easily, but there were many emotions instilled in the air that filled my lungs. I needed to sort out what was going on with myself these days… Was I dreaming? Was I living another life? Was it a life inside myself, outside of myself, or was it actually my whole self, in its totality? The mornings never brought any enlightenment; it felt as if there had been some kind of separation occurring during the whole of this trip, and it had to do with this mysterious stranger that I barely even knew, but seemed to know well, to understand deeply, and, perhaps most importantly, to have this longing to be near. Who was he? And who was he turning me into? Or was he turning me back into who I really was?

Then I started to reflect on the years I had lived, and what they had done to me.

I turned on the radio, and heard a song by U2, "The Sweetest Thing", "A blue-eyed boy meets a brown-eyed girl…"

Within a few seconds, my companion turned the radio off. This time it annoyed me, because I really liked that song.

"Why do you always do that?"

"Do what?" He said, seemingly distracted.

"You always turn the radio off. I liked that song. Don't you think that's kind of rude?"

Lucas chuckled. "Rude, Miss? What do you mean by that?"

"What?" I was confused now. "You don't know what it means to be rude?"

He kept staring straight ahead and wouldn't answer. I didn't know if his silence was just being stubborn, or if he genuinely didn't understand. I kept looking at him, waiting for a response. He finally looked at me, and his expression changed into one of sadness.

"I'm sorry, Miss. Please don't be angry at me. I can see the fire burning in your eyes. Really, what did I do?"

I sighed in frustration. "You turned off the radio and I really liked that song." And as I spoke, I gestured toward the radio on the dashboard. He looked at me, then looked toward the dashboard, and some understanding came onto his face.

"Oh, that. You wanted to listen to that… radio? You think there's anything good coming out of that?"

I sat there, wondering if he was trying to start an argument. "Well, of course. I grew up listening to music on the radio."

My companion seemed to be processing this seriously. I don't understand why he found this concept so hard to grasp, that someone would want to listen to songs on the radio.

"Miss, can you tell me about it?" He sensed my confusion, so he clarified, "I mean, tell me about your growing up, and this radio music you love so much."

I giggled. "Radio music? Okaaaaayyyyy…" I stretched out the 'okay' to express my doubt and reflection upon the topic, because in all honesty, I had never heard it phrased this way before.

"Well, I was born 31 years ago, and during the first 10 years of my life, I listened to a lot of different things, since my family all had different tastes. My mother liked Broadway music, my father liked big band music, and of course my grandma liked music from the era even earlier than that, the first few decades of the past century. My oldest brother wasn't really into pop music; instead, he loved classical, and spent a lot of time playing pieces on the piano. But my other older siblings were into the pop music scene, so I listened to a lot of such songs on the radio and even on records and tapes with our stereo."

My companion made no comment, so I continued: "I really loved The Beatles and The Monkees growing up, and also The Carpenters and John Denver. There was also Abba, Barry Manilow, ELO, Queen, and Styx, and then of course, the Jackson 5 and Michael Jackson."

"Of course?" Lucas had said that as a question, which I thought was weird.

"During the next 10 years of my life, I listened to the radio, but my listening decreased. I kind of stuck with the stuff I grew up with, adding fewer and fewer musicians and bands to what I would listen to. During the third decade of my life, I only liked 1 or 2 new artists. I guess I just lost touch with what was popular. But those songs that I listened to as a young girl shaped me in many ways. I learned rhythm, and I learned to appreciate the beauty of different types of songs and emotions. And many songs had beautiful poetry in their lyrics. Not all of them did, but enough of them did, and those also helped me feel emotion."

I looked at him. "What about you, Lucas? What did you like when you were growing up?"

All I received from him was silence. We had already turned off the main highway onto a country road, so it felt very lonely in the car all of the sudden. He whispered the words, "growing up", then looked reflective. We were winding around roads that were narrower than I had seen in a while, and had to be careful of stray sheep that appeared here and there. No other car was on the road, but if there had been, I don't know how we would have passed each other.

Finally, my companion spoke.

"So, what about this song that you were wanting to listen to. What was it like?"

"You mean "The Sweetest Thing" by U2?"

"Uh, yes, that one from a while ago on the…radio."

"I just love the melody, the way he sings it. It feels just like its name – very sweet."

"I see. And what about its poetry? I mean, its lyrics?"

"Well." I thought for a minute. "Let me think. Well… I guess it's a song about a man whose desperate to stay with the woman he loves, but she is drawing away from him, and he's losing her… It's actually… It's kind of depressing."

My companion grew very quiet, and slowed the car down. When we had come to a place where there were no blind curves, he stopped. Then he opened the door and got out of the car and seemed to be waiting. I had no idea what was going on. He bent down into the window touched me on my shoulder.

"Let's get out of the car and sit for a while, Miss."

I was confused. "Here??" I said loudly. "In the middle of nowhere?"

"Oh, Miss, almost everywhere in Ireland is the middle of nowhere. If you're somewhere, then it's not Ireland anymore. Come on out with you." And he gestured toward the other side of the road, where he sat down, waiting for me.

I had no idea what I had said, but it seemed to have upset him, but he didn't act angry with me, just sad. I liked being around him, and realized I didn't want him to be sad. I really felt strange and didn't understand why he was sad, so I got out of the car and sat down next to him and looked out at the green countryside, dotted with rocks, bushes, and ruins. The wind wound itself along the desolate, lonely landscape that had once been dense with ancient forests. My companion stared for a while, saying nothing, then he took my hand in both of his. When he finally spoke, it seemed as if he had been crying inside.

"I don't understand why you would like a song like this, where a woman is willing to just abandon a man who loves her."

"I just enjoy listening to it, Lucas. Come on. It's just a song. It's not that meaningful to me."

"It's not that meaningful?" He seemed to choke on the idea. "Then why do you listen to it?"

"Because...." And here I was stumped. I had never been interrogated like this over a song. "Because... My goodness, because it's fun to listen to."

"You listen to a meaningless song just because it's fun?" He seemed to be struggling with something. "I don't understand... This seems so... superficial. What has this radio done to you, Miss?"

"I don't understand you, Lucas," I said, trying to pull my hand away from his, but he wouldn't let it go. "What do you mean, done to me? What are you talking about? You don't even know me or how I used to be."

"Miss... That's not true, that's not true," he protested, gripping my hand tighter and shaking his head; then he looked as closely as he could in my face... "I know... I know. And I'm trying to bring you back."

I looked toward the sky in frustration, because my brain could not process his words, they made no sense when I took stock of all of my memories; this man was never a part of my life. I looked at him, but couldn't answer his gaze, because there was a mournful storm inside his eyes. Then he lifted my hand toward his lips and kissed it with a long, lingering pressure... And there was something in that touch that awakened something inside of me that I had never known before, or thought I had never known. There should never have been anything familiar in the touch of those lips on my skin, but they transmitted some kind of electricity throughout my body that felt familiar.

"Miss," Lucas whispered, and his voice seemed to break, "I feel that... I don't want you to be angry, but this radio and the sound that comes out of it, is all worthless to you."

"Can you tell me why you feel that way?"

"This is not about my feeling. It's about yours. My music has never come out of that contraption. It is... Well... Ssshhh... Just have a listen." He released my hand and put his fingers on my eyes. "Close your eyes, Miss. Just listen."

I listened, in the darkness of my closed eyes, and heard the wind blowing, and it seemed to be searching for something, because I could hear, in the loneliness of this place, a loneliness in the air. The wind seemed to be blowing around the empty meadows, searching, forever looking for a place to rest, a place to feel itself, it was looking for its companion, for the forest it had lost, it was crying for her like an abandoned lover… After some minutes of intense listening, with nothing else as a distraction, I could hear its cry. Then… Then I felt something kiss my lips, and my eyes flew open in surprise, because I thought Lucas had abused my trust… but he was sitting next to me, watching me, nowhere near my face. But there seemed to be some kind of expectant expression in his face.

"Come on, Miss. The place I want you to see is just a little further along the road."

We drove a little further, and the countryside was quiet, even more desolate, marked with solemn ruins of the past. I could see up ahead the stone structure of what used to be—

"That was a church," I said, pointed ahead.

"Yes, Miss," the man beside me said. "Ireland has had many of these in the past millennium or so." He pulled up on the road along the place, and stopped. He sat there, and didn't seem to want to move. Finally, he touched my hand, and said, "Come now, let's have a look."

We walked to the stone walls of what used to be a church, which was situated on the top of a great plain. The winds played among the grasses and teased the little flora that still survived; it kept trying to encourage everything on the countryside, to breathe life into the world under its dominion; the only place it could not move was this stone structure, this ancient church; it would hit against its walls, which were immovable, then pass around it and continue its whispering conversation with the countryside. There seemed to be an expectation of something in all this desolation, a waiting, and the church was not privy to everything else that seemed to be understood in the nature across this plain. Of everything around us, it stood alone.

The roof of the church had long crumbled away, and the walls were partially fallen apart, but enough of the walls existed to understand what this place was. The doorway also stood, though just its stone outline; and the back wall, where the Catholic priest would have stood delivering his sermons, also remained intact. It was a small church, just 30 feet by 20 feet. Lucas and I stood at the doorway, then walked inside together.

Grasses grew among the stones, and the natural sky was this church's only light for the rest of eternity. There were tombstones that marked the final resting places of the people who had been part of this church; the names and dates were fading, and the stones were also being overtaken by the grasses and their earth. Lucas looked around at the walls and then down at some of the tombstones. He softly kicked one of them, and some of the stone crumbled at the touch of his foot.

"Oh, Miss, these places make me sad."

"Why? Because they remind you of how history has passed away?"

He smiled at me. "I guess you could say that, in a manner of speaking." He went up to the stone pulpit, where centuries earlier a priest would have delivered messages of reward and damnation. The look on his face was reflective, and the expression in his eyes seemed to be heavy from the thoughts inside. The only brightness was the sun from the open sky, which shone on his hair and turned the brown into a deep blond honey that circled his face.

"This," and he gestured around the two of us, "is not our history, Miss." He leaned on the stone podium, while I leaned against a portion of stone wall that could have been a window. "This came around during the first millennium of man's modern history in Ireland. This did not come from us. I know you've probably heard the history of St. Patrick and may have seen something about him on the first day of your trip. He and the religion of the continent and ancient Rome soak in much of the glory of Ireland. It was a moment of enlightenment, of salvation of souls…" He looked at me for a while.

"Or so everyone thought. But it was a moment of enslavement. Because nothing on this earth belonged to us anymore; this…" As he said that, he spread out his hands, palms up, "This became just a shell, that worked toward something in heaven or hell, and the rules for heaven… they became a very heavy burden to us, Miss."

"We lost any sense of resistance, and finally Ireland was raped of its most precious possession."

Lucas was silent for a while, and he continued looking at me. Then he came over to where I was standing, and stood so close to me, that I felt my back pushing up against the stone wall. His fingers played in the long locks of my hair.

"The Irish forgot how to be men, and in that spiritual humility stood by while the invaders ripped our forests away from our arms, and the Ireland we had known and worshipped…and loved…for millenniums… she was gone from us."

The eyes of my companion were communicating a timeless amount of feeling into me, and I was about to intercede on behalf of history and current Irish culture, when he put a finger on my lips.

"Ssshhh. I know what you are thinking. Don't think it, Miss. Something is still clouding your mind, and I am trying to help you clear it away. These ancient forests, these ancient trees, they had a beauty and inspired a reverence and passion that connected to the soul in ways that these stone structures and their message of other-worldly existence could never do. They had a life within themselves, and renewed themselves, for…if you need to measure things by time, for millenniums of existence. They had been here since before the first two humans lived and consummated their love in the flesh. They were fed by the rivers that lived alongside them, and the rivers running underneath them, and together, these two forces of nature gave life to this world. That was the true life-giving force. But then came men with their twisted logic about the world, and they look half of this force away, and the other half, the waters, alone with nothing to feed that in nature's cycle could give back to them, they eventually began to dry up and to die."

"Miss. Look around you. What is left of this place, this church? Unlike the forests and waters, which were life-renewing, these manmade structures just crumble, and eventually, there is nothing left. It's almost a sacrilege that they were even here."

Lucas bent his head down, and grasped my upper arms, as if he was leaning on me for strength.

"But there is the sorrow. That is what we have left within us. And this sorrow is the deep-seated well that sustains us, gives us life. For as long as we have that sorrow, we know that we still have desire."

I stood there, drinking in Lucas's sorrow. I didn't feel I had anything inside myself to match the breadth of his feeling, so I fed off of what he gave to me in these minutes on the quiet plain, in this lonely, dying church. Then I thought about my grandma.

"My grandma was an atheist. She didn't have a religion."

"Then she was a clever woman," Lucas said, looking at me wistfully.

"She lived very much within her feelings, and her love of nature. I think she would have loved your ideas." And here I paused. "I think… No, I wish… I mean, she should have been the one to come to Ireland."

Lucas reacted with an impatient shake of the head.

"I don't think so," he said.

Now I was surprised and a little angered. I wanted to move around and get into an argument, but Lucas was standing too close to me, and his hands were still on my arms. All I could move was my voice.

"I'm sorry, but why in the world would you say that? I know my grandma, and I know how much she loved Ireland."

"Yes, Miss. And how did you come to know that?"

"Of course, she talked about Ireland and the Irish all the time."

"And how were you thinking and feeling about that?"

I stopped and was confused by this question. But Lucas's expression was so honest, that I felt I needed to answer.

"What did I think and feel… Well… I loved my Grandma. And she made me love Ireland, too."

Lucas was so close to me, that I felt his whole body relax and become calm, and it calmed me, too. He relaxed his hold on my arms, and instead cupped my face in his hands. I couldn't get away from the expression in his eyes.

"Miss, did it ever occur to you, that perhaps you were the one who was meant to come to Ireland?"

I didn't answer him, but my whole body started to tingle in numbness from the sound of his voice.

"Could it be that your grandma was just a messenger?"

Some kind of pathway cleared up in my mind in that instant; as I looked back on all my life's conversations with my grandma, suddenly they seemed to take on a different meaning, a different intent, and this pathway was leading to some kind of purpose that was not logical in my world, was nothing short of irrational.

"Ah, Miss, don't dismiss things that you don't seem to understand."

As he said that, he leant closer to my face and touched his lips against mine. They tasted like pure honey, like the water I had tasted just a few days earlier. I held onto his arms, and felt the soft pressure of his skin, and my inner resistance to this world he was taking me into began to crumble.

He took me out of the church and onto the lonely plain, and we sat down together, watching the winds play in the grasses and the rolling hills. After a while, he stretched out and moved around so he could lay his head in my lap. I looked down at his face, bathed in the sunlight, and it seemed to soak in the rays with a holy light. His blue eyes looked into mine. I began to run my fingers through the soft, brown locks of hair, and his expression softened. The wind was so peaceful that I could hear him breathing, and it sounded like the deep flow of a tranquil river.

"Lucas, can I ask you a question?"

"Of course, Miss."

"Why… Why do you call me Miss?"

He closed his eyes as I started to stroke the skin on his face, feeling the hair that grew along his jawline and on his chin as it tingled my fingers. He seemed to be feeling something beyond this conversation.

"Because…. It's because I have been missing you so much."

I smiled. "Missing me? How is that possible? We have been together constantly these past few days, and we just met."

"Oh no, Miss. That's not true. But soon you will understand what I mean."

Then he sat up and leaned into me, kissing me and gently guiding me to the ground, and I closed my eyes and let myself become immersed in the golden afternoon sun, in the sweet honey taste of his lips.

That evening, since we were so far from any kind of inn or B&B, we again stayed at some lonely farmhouse, where I was only too happy to sleep in the barn. These grasses had begun to take on a comfortable familiarity to my skin, and despite the cooler night air there was a warmth that emanated from Lucas that was like a warm bed. I curled up inside his arms, and was not sure how long I had slept, when I felt myself being lifted.

"Come, Miss," said Lucas, as he put me on his back. "I know this journey is getting a little tiring for you, so I won't make you walk tonight. Just put your arms around my neck, and I'll carry you there;

in my sleep."

I wrapped my arms around Lucas's neck and lay my head on his shoulder and leaned against his back; he grabbed my legs with his strong arms, and walked out into the countryside, where we had been during the day. As before, as we left the single light of the farmhouse far behind, the only things that seemed to illuminate our path were the stars and the moon. When we had gotten to the desolate fields, he let me down. I looked all around us, and everything seemed deathly quiet. I could not even hear the wind. Then, in the heavy silence, I heard an ungodly scream ring out in the night. Out of instinct, I grabbed Lucas's arm.

"My God... What was that?" I cried under my breath. The man next to me was very still, as if it had not affected him at all.

"A banshee, Miss."

When he said that, I nearly fell to the ground, and had to grip his arm for balance.

"Don't worry, Miss. She can't do anything to us."

I could feel my lips lose all their blood, and my body shook.

"Why are we here, Lucas?"

"It's a ceremony, of sorts. Turn around."

When I turned around, there was some kind of natural doorway, a tunnel of trees that had not been there before, that led to some cavernous darkness. Their branches overarched and twisted together, and the path led to something at the end that was unclear.

"What is that?" I asked my companion, although I didn't know why he would know.

"Ah… It's kind of like… a sacred place," he said.

"That's no sacred place I know. It seems scary," I said, and I held back.

Lucas stood in front of me, and looked at me with an infinite sadness in his eyes. The moon tried to fight against the darkness of the blue in those eyes, but tonight seemed overpowered. I just stared into the impassioned sorrow in their darkness.

"Miss," came his voice, rich and pleading, "How do you know you don't know? The issue is not whether you know. The issue is whether you remember."

My breathing became labored; this man was taking me somewhere inside myself that I could not access by my logic, but deep inside I could sense it, I could not deny it, and in the end, I had to admit it.

"Ok, let's go."

We walked through the canopy of trees together, and Lucas had his arm wrapped around my back, his hand on my waist. With each step, the grasses became smoother and richer, more full of life, and the trees became richer in their growth, and I started to hear sounds, strange sounds I had never heard during my earthly existence. I could see small points of light moving around up ahead and along the sides of us, and I whispered to Lucas,

"Are those fireflies?"

He looked around and smiled. "Fireflies? You're meaning the lights?"

I nodded.

He subtly shook his head. "Oh, Miss. Leave yourself behind."

I put my arm around Lucas's waist, because he seemed to be the only thing that was real in this darkness full of shapes and sounds and points of light that did not have a name in the world I had grown up in; even the books of fairytales I had read as a young girl had not prepared me for what I saw. As we came out of the other end of the canopy, Lucas gently encircled me and kissed me.

"Welcome home, Miss," he whispered in my ear.

The world had taken on a luxurious growth that was like a breathable ocean of movement and life. Everything was in darkness, but the shadows were moving, and points of light played around us, and the natural growth of millenniums of ages before humans even knew life surrounded us. My feet, although on the ground, felt as if they stood on air, life in this place was so effortless. The growth beneath me, true to its name, seemed to grow and tickle my feet and legs as I walked. The branches of trees hung down and brushed against my face, their leaves as soft as silk against my skin; there was a moisture to their surface, and it seemed to evaporate into the air as a sweet flavor that I could taste as I breathed. I kept looking at the lights that seemed to be everywhere, creating a music of movement.

"Moonbeams," I said.

Lucas looked into my eyes. "What did you say, Miss?" he said.

I felt a ray of light play across his face and then it moved away, and other points of light danced around us at a distance.

"Those lights… Something like moonbeams…" I shook the craziness out of my head. "No, no, no… That's not possible. Light moves in straight lines."

Lucas kissed me again, as if he wanted to encourage me. "Only if the light is not alive, Miss. Stop fighting against your memory… Come on. I want you to join me."

As we walked within the strangely tangled, growing forest, the creatures called out with insistent songs, and they were all answered; and there was a melody of life around us that had such a beautiful rhythm to it, a subtle urging to live, to feel the sound and the life and to constantly experience growth and renewal. I could feel my breathing becoming even clearer than the previous night, and my heart was pounding with some expectant understanding that this place held some kind of eternal secret… and this man next to me was bringing me closer to it. I held onto his hand, and we walked together.

There was a clearing in the forest, and we came to a place where beyond us a horizon stretched out into the sea and the starlight of the universe.

"Look on either side of you, Miss." I had already looked around, so I stared at him in curiosity.

"On that side are the waters, the life-giving waters of this world, and on the other side is the forest, the trees, which was what these waters lived for. And together, they formed a bond that gave each other life. But look at this bare land. It separates these two, and has done so for too long. In that world where you came from, the waters are also dying, for lack of their lover. How will they ever come back together?"

I stood there, looking at him, as his angelic face and body caught the darkness of the waters and the moving light in the air. I could only breathe in silence. I was trying to find an answer to his question, because there was something dawning inside me; somewhere deep within me something was growing, and I was starting to feel that this man who had suddenly appeared leaning against my car had been waiting for me. I still couldn't completely understand why, and I was frozen in this stare of wonder, breathing through my dry lips.

Then Lucas, standing in front of me, began to take his shirt off, and his bare chest was so close to me, that I touched it with my fingers, and it seemed to move to my touch. It was strong, unresisting, but yet soft and resisting. He moved a step toward me and I put my hand out firmly to stop him.

"What are you doing," I said to him. It was not a question.

"Oh, Miss," he said, with a mixture of amusement and fire in his eyes, "What are you doing. Up with your hands, —" and he said something after that I could not understand.

"What did you say?" I asked.

"I said your name," he said.

"No, you didn't," I protested. "My name is—" And he put his hand over my mouth, and shook his head with an expression of annoyance.

"Stop that," he said, "We're not in that world right now."

He removed his hand from my mouth, then slowly ran his hands down my arms and hands, then, gently gripping my fingers, he lifted them above my head. Then he ran his hands down the skin of my inner arms.

"Keep them up there, Miss."

And his hands gripped the bottom of my night shirt, and slowly pulled it up around my head, up past my arms, and off my body. I stood there, shivering in the moving darkness and light, and Lucas held me against his chest. I could feel the hairs at the top of his chest, and the smooth skin below that, and his heart somewhere deep inside of that, pounding inside my own skin. His hands moved around my skin and I became this unresisting existence. The ground underneath my feet seemed to disappear, and I felt myself moving horizontally. Lucas put his lips to my ear and seemed to say, "Ssssshhhhh," but it grew in intensity and seemed to be the sound of waters rushing up toward a shore, the sound of raging rivers. Then he laid his lips on my lips, and I could feel him coming upon me like a crush of strong waters, and the water entered and rushed to every pore of my soul, even to my fingertips, it was warm and cool, and refreshing, pure and sweet like honey, and I felt myself being pushed down by him, into the earth, deeper into the ground, and he was following me, and all I could do was hold on to his unyielding strength around me... I was drowning, but I felt I could breathe in these waters, and I was breathing more deeply than I had ever done in my human life...

Then a sudden light of dawn lit up the world around me, and I could feel gravity again as I was being lifted up. I flayed with my hands to keep from falling, and grabbed on to something.

"Miss, Miss," I heard somewhere in the light.

I opened my eyes, and I saw Lucas, this strange companion of mine, looking at me. He was holding me in his arms, and my arms were around his neck. I looked at him for a moment without comprehension, then saw the familiar walls of the barn in which we had slept. I could feel my clothes sticking against my skin, dripping with wet.

He wasn't smiling at me, but was looking at me with a serious expression instead.

"It's getting a lot harder to bring you back into the day, Miss."

Then he placed me on the ground where we had slept the previous night.

"Will you be needing any breakfast?"

I realized that I was not in the least hungry, and shook my head. Lucas looked at me and seemed to understand.

"There's a proper answer." He rubbed and patted my leg. "Get dressed, Miss. We have somewhere we're needing to go."

## Chapter 7: The Post-Consummation

We had gotten in the car together, and Lucas was about to start the engine and drive, when I put my hand on his arm.

"Stop. Wait a second."

He stopped and gingerly lowered his hand onto his lap, then stared ahead. "What is it, Miss." And there seemed to be some trembling in his voice. I touched the other side of his face with my hand.

"Look at me, Lucas."

When he looked at me, the blue in his eyes seemed to be moistened by the air of the morning dew. He didn't smile at me, just waited for me to speak.

"Something strange is happening to me."

As soon as I said that, my companion's face relaxed into more of a smile. He turned toward me and put his land on my leg.

"What are you meaning by that," he said, in a mysterious and playful way.

"Come on. I'm serious."

"I have no doubt about that. Tell me your heart, Miss."

When Lucas said things like that, it took me a moment to recuperate my logic. I looked into his eyes, and the dew seemed to have evaporated, and instead was a provocative light. I looked at him for a minute, and played with the beautiful outline of his face, down his soft cheeks and the roughness of his jawline to his chin. I smiled inside myself, then I bit my lips so the smile would not come out and erupt in shy laughter.

"God, you are one handsome man," I said out loud. It came out, I couldn't stop it. Then I blushed. My companion erupted into musical laughter.

"Is that it? I don't find that strange. But if it be true, then it's all the luckier for the eyes that get to see it," he laughed playfully.

"No, that's not it," and I took advantage of the moment to move my fingers through his beautiful brown honey hair instead. "Something strange is happening... Every night."

"Is this so," he said softly.

"Yes. Every day we go somewhere, then we go to bed, but then at some point in the night... I think I'm dreaming this, Lucas, so don't think I'm crazy..."

Just then, the wind picked up and I thought I heard some kind of strange noises. They weren't really birds, and we were not near the sea; in fact, the only creatures around were some sheep that had straggled in from somewhere. They were peacefully walking among the grasses.

"Lucas... Ok, this is hard, because I think I'm crazy, and I'm asking you to not think I'm crazy."

"Miss. Stop babbling and have out with it." Just then he lent forward and kissed me and I could feel some kind of soft wind play around my lips and enter inside me. My companion leaned on his seat of the car, waiting for me to speak.

"I've been having these dreams. But they don't seem like dreams. Every night, we go back to where we were during the day, except everything seems different, and then we end up doing things…. Things I could never imagine myself doing in reality… But it seems so real, and yet… other-worldly. I don't feel like I'm "here" anymore; "here" is evolving into something else. But then, just as I am approaching a moment in this experience where it feels like I am at some point of no return, then… you are waking me up, and everything is real again."

"What is real?" my companion asked.

I looked him in wonder at this question. "That is exactly what I keep asking myself. I'm losing my ability to distinguish it."

"Maybe, instead of losing something, you are gaining something."

"I don't know what that is. These are just dreams." When I said that, Lucas's hand gripped my leg a little tighter. He seemed to be struggling with something.

"Miss," he said, his voice heavy with a sigh, "Who told you that you were only dreaming?"

"Well…." I was confused.

"Then stop thinking you're dreaming, if you are the only one telling yourself that."

"But if what I've – what we've – been experiencing is real, then… I have no idea who I am anymore."

"Ah, Miss. Don't worry. You're getting there." He gently caressed my leg and smiled, but his eyes were piercing me deep inside.

"Wait. Why were you sad just then? When I told you to stop?"

"Ah, Miss, because there are two roads, and they are both moving forward. There's no stopping at this point." He seemed satisfied that he had answered my question.

"Let's be goin' then." And he started the car and drove. But as he drove, I started to think more deeply about who this man next to me was. I looked at the radio and didn't even bother. That music seemed to be a million miles away from me now.

When we had driven for a while, we finally came to where we were supposed to be. I realized that it didn't matter where exactly that was. I just knew that it was a place of beautiful mountains and trees, and I could feel the rivers and lakes. I couldn't see them, but I could feel them beyond my vision. Lucas seemed to sense something, too, or he was sensing something inside me, because he took my hand like he had the day before and kissed it with an unearthly softness that transmitted an electricity through my arm into the rest of my body.

"Ah, Miss. I'm glad that you can feel where you are. It means you are coming back to me."

"Coming back…" I said more as a contemplation, rather than a question. Then I looked at my companion. Whatever was inside his eyes was also inside my soul. I couldn't turn away. "Lucas… I need to know…. Where are you from?"

He smiled in that angelic way, but there was a playful mystery in it. He ran his hand up my arm and onto the back of my neck, and seemed to know just where to touch my skin every time. I was waiting for him to make some kind of misstep, but he seemed to know every single inch of me intimately, and knew just what kind of touch was the most perfect one for any given moment. I couldn't understand how he seemed to know this. But he was quiet, and wasn't answering me.

"Lucas… What kind of man are you? And where are you from?"

He kept sitting there, playing with the hair and skin on my neck. I kept looking at him, and he wouldn't stop staring at me.

"I love your eyes," was all he said.

"Lucas… Where are you from?" I wouldn't let it go. After I asked him that, he released my hand and put his other hand on my cheek.

"Ah, Miss. The same place you're from." Then his eyes became far away, and he almost whispered it. "The same place you're from. Now let's be going there."

The place of tree-filled mountains and waters was somewhat beyond where we were. In fact, he had taken me to a place I had never expected as we got out of the car – an old church. But, unlike the dilapidated ones out in the countryside, this one was still in use.

"Why are we here, Lucas?" I stared at the church as he came around the car to where I was. I was very confused. I had thought we were going to the place of trees and rivers. Somehow, during these past several days, I had come to feel those places were where I wanted to be; I wasn't really interested in visiting these marks of human civilization anymore. As Lucas stood next to me and put his arm around me, I felt an even greater inclination to go to where the nature was wild and breathing, and to feel its waters on my skin. He was watching me, and I felt this strange sensation of floating, and I found myself whispering, as if in a trance,

"Lucas… Can't we go to the forest."

"Yes, Miss, we'll be going there right soon. But we need to do this first. I know your human side needs this before I can come completely inside of you. So just this once, then we'll be finished with this from now on."

I tried to shake myself out of my hazy sensation. I felt like I was losing who I was. "Do this… What are we doing?"

"Why, getting married, Miss." When he said that, he kissed me on my cheek, then released me and walked several steps ahead to the churchyard, then stopped, looking at the church. He just stood there, seemingly waiting for me, but he didn't look back at me. I looked at him and his strong arms and those beautiful locks of honey brown hair that lay tousled upon his head. Then I saw something deeper, a strength and beauty and, maybe most importantly, an intense longing that I follow him… Or perhaps that last part was from myself. I walked up to him and took his hand.

"Ok, let's go."

Inside the church, the air seemed rather dark and smelled a bit of mold. The place had tried to keep itself from aging, but it had aged inside itself in spite of its effort to remain new, and was slowly becoming an artifact of another time. We went up to the minister.

"Mister," said Lucas, "We were wondering if you could marry us today, if you have the authority to do that."

The priest gave us a look mixed with amusement and imperialism. I couldn't get the impression out of my head that he felt the power of his position and felt a quiet superiority to the two strangers that had come into his abode.

"My formal title is 'Father', sir," he said very seriously to Lucas, "I merely request that you give a bit of respect to my position."

Lucas stared at him for a while. "Of course." Then he paused, and said, "*Father…*" and he put a strange emphasis on this word, "Can you be marrying us today?"

"Well, of course I have the authority to perform this ceremony—"

"—Today, *Father.*" And that strange emphasis was put on the title again.

"Of course, if there is some urgent reason for it," and the priest looked at me, and looked down at my torso.

"Urgent reasons there are, but not the kind you're thinking with your mind," Lucas said, and the priest seemed shocked into embarrassment.

"Well, yes. There is a fee, but I can marry you," he said.

"Fine. We'll be paying that fee now." And he pulled the bills out of his pocket and gave the money.

"But I didn't tell you how much it was." The priest counted the money, and looked at Lucas very quietly. "Ok, this is the proper amount. You must have done your research."

"No, I've just lived long enough to know how people reap their rewards… *Father.*" And the two of them stared at each other until the priest became strangely uncomfortable.

"Ok, just wait here for a minute, please."

After being with Lucas for these past several days, the priest's speaking seemed so stilted and formal, and I felt very strange hearing him talk. I shouldn't have, it was just normal speech, but I had grown accustomed to the flowing cadence in my companion's voice; there was an openness and simplicity in its flow, and suddenly I was listening to this other person speak, and his words and thoughts seemed to be dammed up. And then thinking about this reminded me of the word "damnation", and then I remembered where I was, and I started to laugh.

Lucas looked at me as if he knew the joke inside my mind. "Ay, Miss, don't be committing any sacrilege inside here, there's no telling where you'll end up."

I laughed, "As long as I end up with you," I said, half jokingly, and half seriously.

"There's the spirit, my—" and he said something I couldn't understand, like what had happened the previous night in my dreams or waking night life, which actually seemed ages ago now. Then he wrapped his arms around me and kissed me, and the kiss lasted so long that the scent of mold was replaced by something that seemed to come from inside of this man, the invigorating taste and scent of sweet honey. When I felt his lips move away from mine, my eyes were still closed, because I was still standing wherever he had taken me in those moments. Then I heard a voice inside me say, "Open your eyes, Miss," and I opened them to see this man staring at me with eyes that had the intensity of a blue fire, and I didn't want to pull myself away from them.

The priest returned and saw us in our pose, and looked at us as if we had compromised ourselves. Lucas lingered against me for a while, then slowly turned toward the priest, then only after a few seconds of looking at him, he released me.

"So what is this, *Father*," he said.

The priest came up to us, probably hoping that his imperial presence would separate us a few inches further, but Lucas remained very close to me, and I wanted him to be there.

"This is the form," he said, and he held it in between us. "You need to write down your information."

"Our information," Lucas said, looking directly at him.

"Yes, just write your names and addresses, and official ID numbers with your identification cards."

"Lucas, my passport is in the car, I'll go and get—"

Just as I tried to go, Lucas grabbed my arm and pulled me back, although very gently.

"*Father...* My name is Lucas, and this is Miss."

"Is that it? Certainly you have last names."

Lucas put some pressure on my arm before I could speak. "I'm Lucas Smith. And this is Miss Smith."

I almost laughed out loud when he said that. There was something gorgeous in his defiance.

"Both of you are named Smith." The priest looked at us critically. "But Smith is British."

"Then it should make it all the easier for your church to be marrying us, since that is where you're from."

"Mr. Smith, are you questioning the legitimacy of this church?" The priest was trying to stay cool.

"Not at all, *Father*... But Ireland has been around a lot longer than this building."

"I'm well acquainted with the history of this country, as well as the history of my faith. You don't seem to be a very religious individual."

Lucas cocked his head either way at the priest, as if he was puzzling over a strange work of art. "Being religious about certain things is my way," he said.

The priest eyed him suspiciously. "What kind of spirituality do you practice?"

"Ah, an overwhelming one. You can't fathom it."

"Mr. Smith, I am very well educated, and I understand many matters connected to the world's spirituality."

"The world's? Then there's your problem."

The priest was muddled and didn't understand. "I understand the ways of the Lord," he said, staunchly, as if he was marking his territory.

"You know his ways?" Lucas smirked. "How much are you knowing?"

The priest became petulant. "More than you."

Lucas looked at him in silence.

"Is that so."

Lucas's words seemed to echo in the dead silence, and he continued to stare at the priest. There was no wind, but I could hear strange sounds as if they had been carried by some wind. I looked around, and everything, every ornament, was as still as death. Then I looked at the priest, and his face was as pale as death. I had no idea what had struck him like that. The priest's hands started to shake, but when he looked at me he calmed down a bit.

"Miss… Smith… Are you quite certain you want to marry this man?"

I stood there looking at him for a bit, and felt Lucas by my side. The sounds were gone, all that remained was the light filtering through the windows and the unnatural peace inside this church.

"Yes. I wouldn't want anything else."

The priest looked at me with doubt in his eyes, then looked at Lucas.

"You notice how long she paused."

"Excuse me, sir," I interjected, "I wasn't pausing because I was unsure, but because I was trying to find a reason to say no. I found none. Now let's be married."

Lucas kissed me on the cheek, and looked like I had made him the happiest man on the earth. I marveled at this power I had over him, just as he seemed to have power over me. "My beautiful—" and he whispered that strange sound in my ear, the same one he had uttered before. It wasn't the name I had grown up with, but it felt like it was my name, nonetheless. And having said this, the priest married us in a short ceremony that satisfied me, and we were brought together on this earth, in this world, without any earthly names put on paper.

After we left the church, we drove to what was called Wicklow Mountains National Park, Glendalough. Just as I had felt in Killarney, and in these places in my nightly life, there was a calm inside my mind and body, as if this was how the world should be, as if I was… coming home. But that couldn't be, I reasoned within myself. My home was concrete roads, and chain restaurants, was indoor shopping, was traffic noise and buildings. My innocence was tied to well-structured parks with well-worn paths, to playgrounds with swing sets and see saws and merry-go-rounds. I remembered a time when I was young girl, a dizzying ride I took on a merry-go-round, sitting on its steel base, holding on for dear life to the bar. I at first thought it was going to be fun, but then it kept going around and around and around… and my eyes lost their focus, and everything around me kept passing by me with an uncomfortable speed as the older kids kept pushing the contraption to go faster and faster. All the other kids were happy, but I was gripped with a fear and nausea, and all I wanted to do was get off, I was becoming uncontrollably dizzy. I tried to close my eyes, but that just made it worse. I had no control. Even as the ride was whirling around at a dizzying speed, I finally could not control my body, and everything inside came out. The ride abruptly stopped, and the kids all ran off.

From then on, I preferred being on the ground, the soft grasses, the dirt, the mud, or in the gentle streams or waters of natural places. Life in those places never whirled around in an unnatural pace. The rhythm moved, but seemed eternally still. And now Lucas and I, after parking the car, were walking inside a forest that also gave me that calm, eternal feeling.

"This forest has a name, —, but the name you know is a man-given name. I hope you can forget that. The children growing here go by this…" And he said something that I again didn't understand, some language of sound and music and tones that was no language I had ever heard. Lucas looked at me. "Don't worry, my beautiful—, your ability to speak will eventually come back, now that we're together."

Although I didn't understand the meaning of what he had said, like everything Lucas said nowadays, I was just going with its meaning and expecting that everything would be clear to me someday. The two of us walked together in this forest; the afternoon was, as most of the days had been, bragging a sunlit sky and a comfortable temperature with a refreshing breeze. I knew that Ireland was not like this all the time, it couldn't be, but during my time with this stranger who was now my husband, it had been, and I started to wonder if it was just pure luck, or a pure love. I shook those romantic notions out of my head. It had to be a meteorological fluke, I said to myself.

Lucas, who was holding my hand, had been subtly looking at me as we walked along, and right at that moment, he laughed.

"—," saying that strange name of mine mischievously, "What do you think of this weather?"

"You read my thoughts," I laughed.

"Always."

"Well, that's not fair," I childishly complained. "Why can't I read yours?"

I thought I had been joking, but Lucas seemed to take the comment seriously. He stopped and held his head down and sighed. The he got in front of me and took both of my arms, and looked into my eyes. As he looked at me, a tear fell down his face.

"My beautiful—, the ages have not been kind to you. They have ruined your memory." He stepped closer to me, and there seemed to

105

be a shadow in his visage. He sighed again, and I felt a mist inside his breath. "I want you to remember everything. I want you to know everything inside of me, —. I want you to…." and here he spoke a string of sounds that made no sense to my brain, but I could feel some kind of sense of them inside my blood and my nerves tingled everywhere. I felt my breathing become deeper, and when he stopped speaking, he gazed into my eyes, and I gazed into his. I felt he had already met my thoughts deep inside, far past my gaze; but for myself, I was always looking into the depths of his eyes, but still found them unfathomable. But as his voice echoed inside my senses, I saw something inside his eyes that I understood for the first time – Lucas was taking me somewhere, and wherever "home" had been for me in this life, he did not want me to go back.

"Yes, —, I don't want to lose you again. I've been waiting for you. I don't want us to be separated again." His words paralyzed me. I wanted to move, but his hands were still on my arms. He immediately understood my feeling, and released my arms. I put my hand on his face, and felt his human flesh, so soft, and yet strong. The breezes trembled the leaves on the trees that towered above us, and the leaves that had fallen and were beneath our feet also seemed to move, and were speaking that language I had heard only in my dreams during the past few nights. I breathed deeply, and he seemed to drink my breath in with his lips, and his own eyes closed for a second, then opened.

"You're coming back to me," was all he said.

We resumed our walk, but, even though it was still bright everywhere across the world in which the two of us moved, it started to assume the feel of those nightly dreams, that nightly other-worldly life.

As it seemed every day or night, we came to a place with water, this time a beautiful stream. The sunlight shimmered in the waters, and the trees surrounding us seemed to grow more luxuriously, being so close to its waters. I heard the rhythm and its teasing bubbling sounds as the water fell over rocks and kept flowing. I realized for the first time that I hadn't eaten in a long while. I don't think I had eaten regular food for the past 2 days, yet I didn't feel hungry for food. But I did feel thirsty. I bent down to take a drink, and Lucas stopped me.

"Wait, —, I'll give you some in just a moment. Don't be in such a hurry." And he laughed at his own words. The look in his eyes was so playful, that I smiled.

The rest of the forest, except for the sounds of nature, seemed preternaturally quiet. Lucas took his shirt off, and his bare chest soaked in the sunlight that rained down in gentle streams from the openings in the trees above.

"Lucas," I said, looking around, "What are you doing? What if someone sees you?"

"Ah, there's no one who will be seeing us today." And he smiled at me and shook his head. "You have got to stop letting those human notions clutter your mind."

Then he took off the rest of his clothing, and stood before me, waiting. "Come, —, look around you. You've never been shy."

I looked around, wondering what I was supposed to see. All around me were trees standing, exposed to the sunlight and the wind, and I began to shudder, because I was starting to understand, but I didn't want to understand, because there was still something in my mind of who I was now, who I had been in this life… and then I realized I wasn't sure who I was anymore. All I knew was that no one was around us except forest, and here was an overwhelmingly gorgeous man standing a few feet away from me, with bare skin that seemed golden white, and I knew what I wanted to do.

I took my clothes off, a bit self-consciously, and when I stood there before Lucas, also naked, I shivered. He came toward me. "That's the spirit," he whispered, and his whisper caught a breeze and tickled my ears. Then he lifted me up.

"Come in with ya, —," and he set me down in the waters of the stream. I knew my previous self would have fought against this, but for this man, for this moment, what he was doing felt completely right. My body was lying in the waters, and they ran gently around me; my hair played in the water, and I could feel the refreshing warmth and cool that I had felt some nights before touch every part of my skin. Lucas knelt down, then came on top of me, and his skin was completely intertwined in a way with my own that didn't seem possible; the waters rushed around both of us, and his arms came around mine as mine came around his. His lips kissed my neck and then he came close to my face. His honey hair was wet, dripping with the waters of the stream, and I could feel the waters drip softly onto my cheeks. I breathed easily and deeply, and was dying for a taste of these waters that streamed from his skin. He came down on me, and every part of me touched him and felt like it was sinking inside of him, and then his lips came onto my lips, and I felt a rush of strong waters, and I could taste all of his purity and sweetness on my tongue and down my throat, and it came up from my toes, and every part of me below came crashing with everything else inside me, and I could hear Lucas become a powerful voice that encircled me. We were submerged in the waters, and I breathed in these waters, and the stream took us in deeper. I was simultaneously floating and sinking, and closed my eyes… I felt my body stretching out and growing, and Lucas was swirling around me, and I felt myself going deeper into the earth… Then I suddenly emerged into the sunlight with a powerful aspiration; I tasted the waters on my lips as my lover gazed at me, still holding me in his strong embrace. I felt his back with my hands, and he was firm flesh again.

"Lucas," I breathed.

He looked at me with passionate sorrow when I had uttered this. He wasn't speaking to me, but I could feel him asking me, "Why are you calling me this name?"

And I looked at him for a moment. I knew that what I was about to say was the wrong answer. I knew I should never have said it. I was starting to realize for the first time who I was and who he was, and I knew deep down that I should never have said this, but it came out before I could stop it.

"But Lucas is your name."

The gravity of the earth overtook him, and Lucas released himself from me and slowly stood up. I sat up in the waters, and he stood over me for a moment. There was an expression of infinite sadness in his posture. He went to the bank of the stream, and sat there, and even though I didn't want to leave the stream, I got up out of the water and sat next to him.

"Oh, Miss, why did you say that."

When he called me Miss, I felt stricken. I realized that the other name he was calling me was who I was, or connected to who I was supposed to be, and I had destroyed something by calling the person next to me by his human name after this consummation of our marriage. I was just beginning to understand, but then I had reverted to the person I was. I didn't want that person to recede from my memory… Then I realized I didn't know which person I didn't want to lose.

"I'm sorry. I'm sorry."

"Miss, how am I ever going to get you back."

"Why are you calling me 'Miss' again?" I said.

"Because I don't feel that you truly understand your real name, and I'm missing that person with all my soul. I need her… I need you. And I know you need me, too, but you haven't fully grasped who I am – and I can't force you to understand that, either."

We sat there for a while in silence, and I leaned against his shoulder, like a typical human female. I was playing the part I had grown up to play. Then Lucas spoke again.

"I had assumed you were ready to understand. But now I realize you need more time. You need more hunger, more desire to come back to me. I was too eager, because I have loved you so intensely for so long. We have been separated for too long, and the suffering brought upon by this separation has been deep. But then there were forces that had decided that the suffering had gone on long enough, and in mercy had brought you back to the earth. But you were in human form, and needed to overcome this test… You needed to give yourself willingly and with complete understanding of what you were doing. Then we could be reunited. Miss… I wanted you back, and I have been trying to force you to remember and to accept, but now I realize you are not ready to completely accept this, and I cannot force you. And until then, until you fully accept everything on your own, I cannot fully enter into you and we cannot nourish each other's love completely, and we cannot be fully joined together. I forgot that human minds don't grow very quickly. They stay inside their smallness, and don't know things, and then just express their not knowing as a critical non-acceptance."

"You were almost there, you were almost ready to shed that critical doubt and shed your human existence, but I realized I made you come too soon."

There were tears in his voice, as it broke under its own sorrow.

I didn't know how to console him, so I just continued to sit next to him in silence, drying in the summer wind. There was still a large part of me that loved him with a human love, and I could not fathom the type of love he was trying to express to me.

After a while of tranquil sorrow, where we just sat as two lovers who have discovered something that will keep them apart, Lucas got up. He didn't put his clothes back on. He went to the nearby trees and ran his hands along their trunks like a loving caregiver. He touched them like he was caressing baby skin.

"Miss... We made these together." He stared at me, and I felt all the love in his heart. It was not necessary for him to even say it. As he saw that I understood, he nodded his head and his face softened into a wistful smile.

"Don't worry, Miss. We'll come together again, and we will bring everything back."

He came back to where I was, and sat down. We both seemed more comfortable in this way, no more clothes, just enjoying the soil and breeze of the forest. Lucas watched me for a while, then he ran his fingers through my hair.

"Even as a human you are beautiful, Miss. But... I miss you." He choked on those last words a little, and seemed to fight back some painful notion, which he finally expressed.

"Tonight you were going to come with me for good, but that can't happen yet. And I am afraid that, when the time does come when you are ready, you will have completely forgotten me, and will not come." He stared at me for a few seconds.

"I'm going to do something to make sure that doesn't happen. We have already been married in heaven since many ages ago, and now on earth. I want to give you a gift as part of that. I'm going to sing you a song, in the style that you understand as a human. When I know you are ready to come back to me, you will hear me singing again… and, the spirits above and below us willing, we will be together again."

I was filled with a sadness at his words, but I didn't know why. There was part of me that was relieved to be sitting here, next to this handsome man who would be a part of me for the rest of time, but then there was another part, that darkness I had not completely accessed yet, that told me that this human form was nothing compared to what he really meant to me, and that my human form meant nothing to him… he wanted something deeper.

When he sang the song, his voice was more beautiful than when he had sung before, and I realized he had been suppressing the full power of its beauty. It was soft and full of yearning, and there was a depth of strength and desire in its low notes, a human masculinity, but then a feminine tenderness in its lovely range. He was not out to prove any human measurements of manliness, because he had an endless well of confidence that could not be diminished. He expressed his song as he had expressed his regret just a little while earlier – with love and sadness… and the message in the poetry was a letter to me.

When he had finished his song, the sun had started to set. He moved behind me and whispered in my ear, "I hope you enjoy this, Miss," and with his fingers he softly touched my back, caressing it while barely touching it, and it made me sleepy.

I said in my half-drowsy state, "But I have nothing to give to you, Lucas."

He whispered in my ear, "Sshh…" and it felt like the rush of waters. "Just come back to me. Don't leave me, Miss. Please don't leave me alone."

I needed to say something else to him. "I loved your being inside me, Lucas… I somehow felt that I wanted you to always be inside me like that."

"I will be, Miss. I will be."

He smoothly caressed me, and I felt so sleepy, I lay down on the ground. He then wrapped his body around mine, my breasts covered by his left arm and hand, and my stomach by his right, and his legs were around my legs. He kissed my shoulders, and sang in a whisper, "Good night, Miss…" and the lullaby-like tone put me to sleep.

That night I dreamed of Lucas in two different ways.

In my first dream, the stream we were near had become a deep river, and I was swimming upstream from where we had been. It was night, and I could see a golden white glow downstream, and realized it was Lucas. He was sitting on the bank, watching me, and seemed to be waiting for me. I slowly swam to where he was, then held on to his strong thighs where he was sitting. His thighs parted, and I came closer to him. The waters of the river had been just normal water, but I kissed his skin, and the water dripping down his body tasted deliciously sweet; all I wanted to do was kiss the wetness on his torso and chest, as I held on to his legs. Then he came into the water with me and, encircling me, turned me against the bank of the river… Then he spent a long time rushing inside of me like soft water, and he kept coming inside me like the current of the river, and all I could do was breathe him in and feel the honey sweet of his waters everywhere inside of me.

In the second dream, he watched over me as I slept, and gently wept. Then at some point he turned into water and sank into the ground around me.

In the morning, I woke with the sunlight all around me. Leaves and dirt were mixed with my hair, and the ground around me felt damp to my touch. The stream near me bubbled quietly. It took me a moment to remember where I was. I sat up, and realized I was naked. My clothes were in a pile a few feet away from me. But, perhaps most surprising to me was that I was alone. Lucas was gone.

## Chapter 8: Return to Civilization

I looked around, wanting him to be there. The forest in the morning was glorious. The trees stretched into the light of the sky like an over-arching heavenly dome, and the music of the morning nature was subtly coming to life. The stream near me gurgled softly, and birds high in the boughs above me sang to each other, while the wind carried their song to the rest of the forest and awakened all of the life that spread out beyond this small space on the earth where I lay.

I lay back down for a moment, remembering the song that Lucas had sung to me. I could still feel him inside me, hear his voice and feel his skin, and that most peculiar sense, I could still feel who he was inside me, his thoughts and his spirit. I could feel it fading, but my love for this man who had been a stranger but who within the last few days had become so intimate with me was keeping him inside me. I couldn't lose him. I realized within myself that I had said something wrong, I had made an error of judgment that had somehow deeply wounded his soul and made him retreat... But where he had gone, I was not so sure. I felt he was still with me somehow, but, to my human sense, which was becoming the dominant force inside my body again, he had disappeared. I felt helpless.

I grabbed at the moist earth near me, and dug my fingers into the ground. I felt like he was there, and here I was, desperately trying to bring him back.

"Lucas... Please don't be gone," I said, and I just lay there, naked, the sun streaming onto my skin, the tears streaming down my face and falling onto the ground. I thought about his honey brown hair that was so soft to my touch, and his easy laughter. I remembered his caring voice, and our open conversations; I could feel his touch on my skin, and he had touched me almost everywhere, so my skin was still yearning for the continued touch of his fingers. I loved that face, which was so soft, and yet manly, with the roughness along his jaw and on his chin. Most of all, I could not escape those eyes. But those were still with me. I turned onto my back, and there they were, staring at me in the blue of the morning sky. I reached up and caressed his imaginary face, and just lay there for a while, staring up into his eyes.

Finally, I got up and looked at my clothes. I had no inclination to put them back on. I stood there, not wanting to leave, thinking that if I just waited here, waited for an hour, or a day, or even, drastically, a year, Lucas would return. But I had enough of my inner sense of him remaining to realize that for him a year was meaningless. I was not sure how long it would be before I saw him again, if ever. After waiting there for over an hour, I finally decided to leave. I took a few steps away from the place that I had last been with Lucas, then something within urged me to look back – and look back I did.

Where I had been lying, in the place where I had cried my tears of loss, there was a tiny plant that had just started emerging from the soil. It had not been there an hour earlier, and I stared at it as if were a memento of an already distant memory, and for the first time in the past few days I thought about my grandma again. Then the pain of hunger in my stomach awoke me to a human need that I had not felt in a while…and I walked out of the forest.

As I walked out of the forest and toward my car, people who had come to the forest stared at me in wonder. I must have looked a frightful sight to them, but everything had felt natural to me; the dirt caked on my skin, the mud and leaves in my hair, the fact that they were wet, and perhaps most of all, that I was wearing no clothes… but my physical state felt natural to the existence I had been experiencing these past few days. Perhaps there had been something

116

inside of me growing out, and it was shedding the material need of this façade that was so corruptible and temporary. I ignored their stares, and walked the rest of the way to my car naked. There was still something in that forest that was pulling me in, and deep inside myself, the narrow-minded reactions from these people didn't matter to me.

As I drove from the forest, I realized I needed to find a hotel, so I found a place in the Wicklow area, an extremely comfortable-looking hotel. I looked at my body, and realized that this place, this civilization, would never accept my arrival in this natural form, so I fished in my suitcase for a dress and just put it on without anything else except my shoes. There was nothing of Lucas's in my car – he had only ever had the clothes on his back, which nightly he had found a way to wash in waters, and those were gone.

When I checked into the hotel, I first ate something, just a simple meal, to acclimate myself back to regular food again. I sipped the water. It tasted bland and disappointing. I called the waiter.

"Yes, ma'am?"

"Do you think I could have some pure water?"

"Excuse me?"

"I want some pure water. This water doesn't taste right."

"But this is pure water. Perhaps you would like a different type. Wait for just a minute."

The waiter went away and came back, with a not-so-hidden appraisal of my physical appearance.

"Have you been camping, ma'am"?

"Camping?" I was confused. Then as his eyes looked me up and down, I understood his meaning. "Well, no. But I have been out in the natural elements."

That seemed to satisfy him, and he put the water in front of me. I looked at it. It was a plastic bottle. I stared at it, uncomprehending for a few seconds. I picked up the bottle, and looked at the water through the murky film of plastic. I twisted off the cap, which opened with a little popping noise, and I looked inside at the water. It smelled bland. Then I took a drink. It was bland.

The waiter noticed my reaction, and said with some consternation, "Is it okay, ma'am?"

I didn't look up at him. I just kept looking at the water, trapped in this manufactured bottle. I just said under my breath, "It's fine, it's fine. It's okay... It's okay." The waiter seemed satisfied. I kept looking at the little bottle of water, and thought about my first taste of those drops from Lucas's fingers...

"Oh, Lucas, where are you?" I whispered. And I hung my head and I cried.

After that, I hardly had any appetite. I just ate a bite or two more, paid my bill, then went upstairs to the room. The place was immaculate, and the bed was soft and white. There was a part of me, the human part of me that had not yet fully returned inside myself, that recognized that this bed was very comfortable, but I did not feel it.

I ran the water into the bathtub, and, stripping off my dress, I got in. In the past, I would have run hot water, but this time it was cool, with just a little bit of warmth, just it had been each time Lucas and I were inside the water together. The dirt floated off my skin and

118

hair, and I felt water on me as if I were feeling Lucas with me all over again, and my breathing became clear for just a brief second as I remembered the feeling of him inside of me. I submerged my head in the water and tried to feel everything again, but the water got inside my throat and started choking me. I had to get my head above the water, or I knew I would die, and I couldn't do that. There was something that needed to happen in my life, but it wasn't this, in this small bathroom in this hotel room. I lay there in the water, and after a while, I fell asleep.

I was inside a dream, floating in water, and I felt like it was carrying me gently to the end of the world. The water was the icy cold of the ocean, the cool of the sheltered shore, the comfortable, warming coolness of the stream, the cool refreshing vitality in the fountain coming from the earth, and the warmth of the deep springs down inside. The water caressed my skin, softly understanding every part of me; and the way the water entered inside of me, I was not choking, but instead I breathed more clearly, and was awakened to a vitality that I had never had in all my years before on earth. It seemed like I was given existence by this water, and all it wanted to do was keep coming and giving me life; in turn, I gave something back to the waters, but what I was or what I was supposed to give was still unclear, because in these dreams, I was still just a human. I felt inside myself that I had come closer to something about my identity than I had ever known before, but I had not reached it; and now that truth was far away from me now. And so these waters, while they were a protective, warm embrace to me, also became something where I felt lost.

"Miss, Miss, are you okay?"

I could feel someone's hand under my head, and another hand was gently patting my cheek.

"Lucas?" I whispered out of the watery darkness. I reached out of the water and held on to the figure hovering over me. It was a boney arm.

My eyes flew open, and I saw a woman looking at me with worry on her face. She was dressed as cleaning staff.

"Who? Who are you?" I said, confused.

"I'm the cleaning service, Miss. I've come to clean the room. But it doesn't seem like you've really used it."

"But I was just taking a bath. I don't understand…" I was trying to clear my mind. "Don't you just come to clean once per day?

"Yes, ma'am. That we do." Now she was confused. "I'm here for the late morning cleaning."

"Late morning cleaning?" I looked around. "What day is it? Didn't I just get here?"

"Why ma'am, you've been here overnight already."

I completely woke up to where I was, and sat up. Then I got up and got out of the tub right in front of the cleaning person. She seemed a little surprised.

"Miss, I'll leave and come back later if you need a little privacy."

I turned toward her and looked into her eyes. "I don't need anything. You do what you need to do."

I started to walk out of the bathroom, and the woman called to me.

"Miss, please dry yourself. You'll catch your death of cold." She held out a clean white towel to me. I just looked at it.

"I don't need anything." And I walked toward my suitcase. I loved the feel of the water on my skin, and longed for it to remain, but I knew that eventually it would naturally dry off. I only had one other dress, and put it on, because I still didn't feel comfortable with the feel of all the other clothes on my skin, although eventually the need to wear them would return to me, as I became more reacquainted with all the feelings and tendencies of human civilization. I thought about Lucas that night at the bottom of the cliff next to the ocean, and how he had moved a little ways away from me to accommodate my sensitivities. He called those sensitivities "American", but now I realized that at the time he was hiding the full scope of what he was trying to communicate. He meant "human" sensitivities. And I had stupidly stood aloof from him and kept my clothes on, as some kind of moral protection. I wished I could go back to that night in my dreams. I would take everything off and throw it into the sea, and go to him completely. He had been waiting for me, and he was patient. And now he was waiting again for me to strip off something deeper, something I still couldn't fully access, but I could feel it deep inside somewhere, like a secret itching at my consciousness, waiting to break through.

"I'm going to find it, Lucas," I said inside myself.

I looked at the things I had brought into the hotel room. I pulled out my map of Ireland and sighed. The country on the map was green, but crossing it were roads, and dotted around were cities and towns. I put my finger on it and traced the little lines that cut up the beautiful country like a knife, and I thought about the nights that Lucas and I had crossed grassy fields barefoot. I could feel the tingle of those grasses on the underbelly of my feet in my memory, their strong coarseness and smooth feel, like Lucas's face. My finger moved to the rivers and followed their paths on the map, then touched the waters along the shore. I felt everything within me go numb, and I closed my eyes, breathing in the memory of his waters.

"I need a drink," I gasped.

The cleaning women came out into the room.

"Miss? Did you say something."

"I need a drink."

The women became concerned. "Just wait here. I'll get something."

She came back after a few minutes, and tapped me on the arm. "Miss. Here is your drink."

I turned around, and I looked at her outstretched hand. It was a plastic bottle of water. I stared at it, and I started to feel everything inside of me go dry. I reached out for it, my hand shaking. As I took a hold of it, the worker let it go, and it felt like a brick in my hand, and it fell to the ground with a dead thud. Tears started streaming down my eyes, and I started sobbing in gasps.

"Miss... I will leave you alone," and she hurried out of the room.

I knew that it was somewhat meaningless at some level now, but I decided to finish up my trip by going to Dublin. I kept this hotel, since the town was smaller, and the hotel so comfortable, but I went ahead and took a bus into the city. The first day of travel, I went to the home and museum of George Bernard Shaw. I was the only visitor, which I supposed indicated something about the level of readership of this once esteemed author, but the advantage was I could enjoy the entire home by myself. A lady met me at the first floor and explained some things, including the kitchen at that level. After that, I went up the stairs on my own, venturing around and reading the points of interest. The previous me, the woman of just over a week earlier, would have been fascinated by this place; but the current me found the rooms small and limiting. I realized that, to humans, this lifestyle was considered comfortable...

I caught my breath. It was hard to breathe in that place.

The next day I went to St. Patrick's cathedral, which was a very popular tourist attraction. As soon as I entered, I heard a chorus of voices; it was an all-boy choir being led by a priest. Their voices resonated inside the entire church, and echoed in the uppermost boughs of the gothic ceiling. I looked all around, and felt awed by the architecture. The arching supports, the tall height that was far beyond my reach; I knew, at some level, this was meant to give people an impression of the power of God and heaven, and the voices of the boys were all around me, trying to uplift my spirit. I kept looking up at the ceiling, and started searching for the beautiful blue sky that I had often seen reflected in Lucas's eyes; yet all I could see, the higher the ceiling was, the darker and further it was from the heavens. I didn't want to forget those eyes, so I went out of the church, and when I did, the chorus of voices was shut out by the closed door, and all I heard was the traffic noise of Dublin.

The next morning, I got my stuff ready, ate breakfast, and went to my car. I needed to drive the width of Ireland, back to the Shannon Airport, and I only had a few hours before I needed to check in for my flight. I thought I had given myself enough time, except I had accidentally locked my keys in the car. There they were, lying on the driver's seat. Just when I despaired of being able to go, a dark-haired, friendly-looking Irishman suddenly appeared. I had no idea where he had come from.

"What's up, Miss?" he asked with a smile.

With a tinge of stress that was more like my former American self, I said, "I locked my keys in my car, and I have to drive all the way across Ireland to the Shannon Airport."

He looked inside my window, and with another smile and twinkling in his eyes that seemed so unique to the Irish, he said, "Don't worry, Miss, we'll be getting it out for you."

A minute later, some other man joined us, and also joined the conversation, and he said, "What's up here?"

"This Miss locked her keys in her car."

They conferred with each other, and made a solution.

"Just wait for a minute, Miss. We're getting a wire."

I watched these two strangers, whose names I would never know, work diligently and with a manner of humor as they played with the wire to get it through the top of the car window, then down toward the lock. They seemed to look at this as more of a bit of fun than a favor, and I stood there laughing inside at their sweet countenances. Finally, after about 15 minutes, they got the door unlocked, and were as genteel and gracious about it as I never could have expected.

"There you go, Miss. Now off to the airport. You should get there in enough time."

I had no idea how these two men just showed up out of nowhere and were the perfect help for my situation, but beggars don't ask questions of the good luck that passes their way. So I got into the car and, map in hand, I started my morning trek across Ireland, thinking that I still had enough time to get to the Shannon Airport and make my flight.

I drove out across the country, and I was able to experience the beauty of the Irish land one more time, even though I knew it was missing one of its vital elements – the rich forests that used to cover the hills. Still, the green hills were a wonder to see, and I got lost in their beauty. Then I literally got lost. I had followed the map to the letter, but then, after I had driven a while, I found that a sign I had passed an hour earlier came up again. I had somehow circled back and was redriving the route. I stopped at the sign and looked at the map, trying to reorient myself. I remembered what Lucas had said about maps in Ireland – they aren't going to get you where you need to go. As I remembered his beautiful laughing voice saying this, I calmed down and just let the situation come to me as it would.

I got back in my car and started driving again, and this time somehow the route worked itself out. I finally arrived at Shannon Airport, and returned the rented car on time.

The flight, however, was a different story. By the time I had gotten there, it had already left. Thankfully, my ticket had insurance on it, so they just rearranged for the next flight back – 24 hours later.

Having already returned the car, I just relaxed and decided to practice some patience. Shannon Airport was not very large, so I sat at some seats and settled in for the wait. During that time, a variety of people from different countries came through the airport, including 2 Frenchmen who had gone cycling and were packing their bikes for the flight, and a group of Germans who must have been having a very interesting, harmonious discussion… But since I only knew English, I could understand almost none of the conversations that had occurred. As I listened to these foreign languages, I thought back upon the sounds that Lucas had uttered to me, which were not like any human language, and yet they had started to feel familiar and comforting inside me. I tried to remember what they were, but they were so strange and other-worldly, they had already started to fade.

The next day, I left Ireland. I had no plans in the future for returning, I had no idea what the future would be. Nevertheless, I had a desire to return, and I expressed that desire in the calendars I would buy for years after this visit, where every month showed pictures of this country that I knew was a part of me, and for more than just because my grandma had loved it.

A week after I returned from Ireland, I went, as I had planned, to China and started a different life there. I settled into Beijing, a city of concrete, and the lack of breathable air and drinkable water pushed whatever was left of my sensations with Lucas to a place in my mind that for quite a few years I could not access, making him disappear in a way that seemed more final than his departure in the forest.

## Chapter 9: The Voice

The years passed by just as they often do in an adult life; more quickly than in childhood and with relentless force. I could not reel them in, I could not make the seasons pause so I could deepen my enjoyment of all the moments that were the most beautiful. The tenacity of spring blossoms gave way to the hazy laziness of summer, which eventually turned into the fiery oranges, reds and golds of autumn; but just as I was enjoying each season, winter came and everything died again. The white snow became a shroud that covered my memory of Lucas more deeply with each year, another layer of forgetfulness concealing my youth and pushing me into the sorrows and realities of middle age, which was the stage that came before the mental and physical decrepitude of being old.

Fifteen years had come and gone since I had been in Ireland the first time, and I had not returned. Every year I made a wish to see that beloved country, but every year, the fact of poverty and practical constraints kept me away. I had spent most of those years in Beijing, China, and the dry seasons and lack of nature in that metropolis had evaporated almost all inner sense I had had of that time in Ireland.

After all that time, however, I decided that I had been in China long enough, and I returned to America, thinking that I would finally settle down there. Before I did, however, I had to take another trip to Ireland. It had been 15 years, and through all those years the details of my trip there had started to take on a more abstract sense, but the desire to be there had never diminished.

Thus, in October of that 15th year, I found myself on another airplane, heading for that green country on the other side of the Atlantic Ocean. Just as before, I landed in Shannon Airport, and I rented a car. This time, however, instead of Bed and Breakfasts, I went to hotels that I had planned in advance. I decided to revisit many of the places I had been before, and add some places that I had not yet seen.

After the first night, I came down and ate my breakfast, and had my stuff ready to pack in the car for the next leg of my trip. When I went outside, I saw a figure leaning against my car, and my breath caught in my chest for a second. As I got closer, however, I realized it was a young kid, maybe 16 or 17, with bright blonde hair that covered his head in playful swirls, reflecting the brightness of the sun. He was thin and spritely, and when I came up to the car, he looked around, then looked back at me, smiling coyly. His eyes were bright blue, as bright as the morning sky. I must have looked serious, because he quickly became apologetic.

"Oh, I'm sorry ma'am, is this yours?"

"Well, yes and no."

He looked at me in confusion, then I explained, "I don't own the car. It's a rental I'm using for my trip."

He laughed very easy, somewhat childish, but very free and beautiful laughter, and said, "Oh, I'm sorry, Miss, I was waiting for someone, I'll go somewhere else." And he walked off, almost tripping boisterously in his youthful innocence. I could hear him singing a sweet song to himself, and his voice uplifted my heart.

I should have been disappointed that it was not who I had hoped, but something about that boy made me feel very comfortable and happy inside. I went to my next destination, which, as it had been before, was Killarney National Forest.

Sadly, the old man who had been there originally was no longer alive, and the wagon drivers no longer interacted with me with the same flirtatiousness as they had when I first came to Ireland. As I looked in the mirror of my hotel room, I realized, with some dismal resignation, that I was growing old.

That night, I slept well. Unlike the last time, I was not awoken at night for any excursion out into the Killarney forests and lakes. Even as I thought about the details I could remember, everything about that night seemed to take on the nature of a fanciful dream. But I had come to expect that these types of things would no longer happen to me. As I had gotten older, my dreams at night had slowly been disappearing.

The next day, I wanted to leave, but for some reason I felt impelled to stay in that area; I had over-planned this trip in some ways, and decided I needed to allow some of my feeling to guide me, or it would be nothing like my former trip. I ventured around Killarney during the day, then in the evening I went into a pub where they had a live performance.

I was a little shocked when the person came onto the stage, because he looked so familiar. There was something about his face that looked like the boy who on the previous day I had found leaning against my car. He had ferociously blonde hair that was wavy, but also a bit spiked. He was as friendly as a sunny day in summer, and his songs were light and fun. The patrons seemed to like him a lot, and I have to admit his personality was charming. I didn't drink alcohol, but I got into the spirit of singing that seemed contagious; the boy loved singing uproarious Irish songs that had no place on a Sunday morning mass.

After a few hours, I left the pub and was walking to my car, when I heard a voice:

"Miss. Miss!"

I had to catch myself, because there was something in his voice that was so familiar, so I turned around. It was the performer. I immediately laughed at myself – of course, people who come from the same country will have the same voice, I thought to myself; I had probably already heard it in the talk of the other Irish boys during the first few days of my trip. I stood at my car, wondering what this boy wanted.

"Where are you going?"

I laughed at his strange question, which at the same time seemed familiar, and said, "I'm calling it a night. I'm going back to my hotel."

"If you don't mind, can you drive me somewhere?"

I laughed again, but a bit nervously this time. "Well… How old are you?"

"Eighteen, ma'am." He had said it so sincerely and respectfully, that my fears of being with a stranger were immediately assuaged. Moreover, he was lanky just like that younger boy had been, so I figured there was no danger. I let him get his guitar, and he got in the car next to me.

"So, where should I take you?"

"I'll give you the directions, ma'am."

He had me driving quite a circuitous route, and before I knew it, we were out in the countryside. By the time I realized that this drive was actually going to take a while, I couldn't say anything, because we were so far from civilization that I couldn't have brought myself to abandon this boy on some lonely country road. Besides, he was a wonderful companion for this little stretch of time on a trip that I realized was going to be a very lonely one. He talked in a bubbly way about his singing at the pub and Killarney itself, and seemed to love life. I asked him some questions about his family, but he wouldn't answer. Perhaps he had been taught to be cautious about giving out personal information, which I could understand in this day and age. It was really hard to fully trust anyone. The irony of that thought struck me, however, as I realized that both of us had ventured out into the countryside in this car together, and there was a high level of trust being practiced on both sides.

When the boy indicated that we were nearing the destination, I looked ahead and saw that we were close to the coast. He had me stop the car at a very lonely spot, and for a moment I couldn't believe that this was where he wanted to go.

He breathed deeply. "Ma'am, isn't this wonderful? I never get out here, since I don't have my own way to get here. Let's go."

He got out, and started walking toward the cliff. I got out, and caught up with him. We walked to the edge of the cliff. The waters of the ocean were black under the night sky, and they moved and roiled in the October winds. The stars of the night sky spread out over and above us and the ocean in a dazzling display of light. He stood there looking at everything for a while, then he sat down. He patted the grasses next him.

"Come on, Miss. Enjoy the view."

I was confused. Had he had me drive for over an hour, all the way out to this solitary spot, just to sit for a while?

"Did you want me to get your guitar? Do you want to play some music?"

He laughed, and his tingling laughter reverberated in our little space, while the rest of the infinite space roared with the deep sounds of ocean.

"No, Miss. That music is nothing compared to this. I don't get out here enough, and it's great just to have a listen. Don't you agree?"

I laughed, but more in an amazed and humorous shock at this boy's innocence and temerity. He had had me drive all the way out here to listen to the ocean. I looked at him, and chuckled inside myself at his wonder-filled pleasure, then went ahead and sat down next to him. The moonlight glowed on his white skin as he watched the waters in silence. I also went silent, and just listened to the waters. I could hear them crashing against the cliff and the deep movement beyond that. I remembered how icy cold those waters had been, once upon a time. Neither of us spoke for a long time, and the constant rhythm of crashing waters drew me into a soft, hypnotic state. I could see out of the corner of my eye that the boy next to me had started looking at me, and was staring for so long that I finally turned toward him. His eyes were the deep blue of the night ocean.

"What do you think of that, Miss," he said, in muted tones.

"It's beautiful," I said.

"I'm glad you think so."

Just when I had started to be more lucid in my judgment and think it weird that a young boy had had me drive him out to the coastal cliffs just to enjoy the scenery with me, I woke up. I was in my hotel room and it was morning.

"Ok, that was strange," I said to myself. "Ireland is bringing back some strange notions."

I shook the notion out of my head and moved on to my next destination. Since I had already gone out on a peninsula and seen the coast, I tried to instead find that place where I had been before, which had provided such pure, sweet water. I remembered that Lucas had driven me that day, so I had no idea exactly how to get there, so I took my best guess of where to get off the highway – and my guess was wrong. I did get out into the countryside, and I did see a lot of sheep – and had even had to navigate around quite a few of them on the roads – but I could not find that place anymore. Finally, I stopped my car when I realized I had not seen any road signs for a while, and decided I was lost out in the middle of the countryside. I looked at my map, and knew it was as useless as my own sense of direction. I sat there in my car, wondering how I was going to get back onto the highway. Suddenly, there was a little tap on the passenger side window. I looked in somewhat of a numb shock. There was a guy standing there, looking in the window, and he looked a little older than the last boy I had been with, yet he looked almost the same. I rolled the window down. The guy was smiling at me.

"Um… Miss… You've chosen a strange place to park yourself." And he laughed at his own words; his eyes shown in the sunlight a bright blue, and his face was as bright as the afternoon light. I laughed in spite of my situation.

"Well, yes. I mean, I am not parked. I am lost. I was trying to find a place, but I ended up here."

"Ireland's roads are tricky, ma'am. They'll take you, not where you meant to go, but sometimes where you're meant to be."

I laughed. "Is that so? So I'm meant to be lost?"

"I don't think you're lost, Miss. I found ya, didn't I?" And he smiled so openly and beautifully, that I couldn't argue his point.

"Well… I had *meant* to go somewhere I had visited before, a sheep farm that had a café that…" I paused. "Well, that had drawn water from a stream that was pure and sweet." I laughed at myself. "I have been driving all over these country roads just to have another drink."

The guy did not laugh, but looked at me with piercing interest. "Have you now." He looked into the distance, then opened the car door and got in. I looked at him in surprise.

"Don't worry, Miss. I'm going to help you find that water. I know these parts very well. Just drive where I tell ya."

I looked at him for a minute. He was a little more grown than the last boy, and was a little more muscular, but he was still just a boy in some ways. I decided to trust him.

"By the way, how old are you?" I asked him.

"Oh, I've just turned 20," he said.

I knew it couldn't be the other boy, but I was surprised at how these males looked so similar to each other. I had a sudden thought of there being a genetic factory somewhere. The guy must have sensed something, because he laughed, and said,

"Miss, what are you thinking?"

Embarrassed to admit that idea, I laughed, and shook my head. "Oh nothing," I said.

After a minute, I started reflecting on this odd stranger, and I did have a question.

"Actually, since you asked, I had a question."

He laughed. "For me? Go ahead. Oh, and Miss, take this curve up here."

"Ok… But about that question… Do you have any brothers?"

"Do I have any brothers? Well no, not to my thinking. Why do you ask?"

"Well, it's just…" And I sighed, because it felt strange to even be saying this. "It's just that I've been in Ireland some days now, and I have seen 3 guys, you and two others, who look so similar. You are all different ages, but… Just forget it. You probably think I'm insane."

"I never said that, and I certainly don't think it," he said, with a very serious tone.

"Well, I think I'm insane."

"No, Miss. Never think that. Maybe you just don't know what you're seeing."

I chuckled. "I know what I'm seeing. I'm seeing double. No, I'm seeing triple." And I laughed. But the stranger next to me didn't laugh. He just silently looked ahead.

"Take this other curve around here, then we'll go down into an area with a stream," he said.

When we got to a stream, I parked the car nearby. The guy got out, but I just sat there for a while, thinking that, if I wasn't insane, this trip was turning into an insane situation. I was getting too old for weird games like this, and something weird was definitely going on.

Suddenly, the guy opened my car door and was leaning on the frame.

"Come on, Miss. I think this is the water you're looking for."

I just sat there, a little perplexed, wishing I could just get back on the highway and go to some easy-to-find tourist spot where I wasn't in some lonely place in the middle of nowhere.

I heard a sigh, and looked up at the stranger. There was an immense sadness in his face, and his eyes seemed... glazed with tears. It tore me out of my critical reverie, as I started to wonder about what had made this guy so serious and sad all of the sudden.

"Come on, Miss," he said with a youthful pleading, and timidly touched my arm. A rush like electricity went through me from that touch, and I blushed.

"Ok, ok," I conceded.

We walked for a few minutes, then we came to a stream. It was not in a forest, but rather ran through a ravine that carved a tender path through the countryside. The water was not coming from out of the earth; the stream itself was very small in comparison to that previous one I had known with Lucas. Still, there seemed to be a childish purity in the way the guy urged me toward it. He bent down and put his hands on the waters. I went next to him and bent down. The sun shone on the golden, blondish-brown locks of hair around his face, which was still as white and as soft as a young boy's face. As he felt the water with his hands, his eyes were closed, and he seemed to be humming some song to himself. I couldn't catch what it was, but I felt I had heard it before. I reached down to take some water myself, but the guy softly stopped my hand and opened his eyes.

"Wait, I'll do that for you," he said, looking at me. I was amazed at the deep blue in his eyes, like rich turquoise. He took some water in the cup of his hands, and stood up, smiling at me and holding his hands out.

I slowly stood up, and looked at him with a critical heart. He didn't seem crazy, but perhaps he was crazy? The boy seemed to sense my reluctance, and, while he continued to stand there with his cupped outstretched hands, he looked pensive, almost crestfallen.

"I'm sorry, but this is just highly peculiar," I said, matter-of-factly. "You are just a young—" and I stopped. I shed the words I was about to say, I shed my resistance. I took his cupped hands in my own, and bent down to drink from them. His skin was so smooth, yet his hands were firm. Then my lips and tongue touched the waters in his hands, and I tasted the sweetness of honey.

I abruptly woke to a tapping near my ear. I was inside the rental car. I looked out the window, and a policeman was tapping on the window. I rolled it down.

"Is everything okay, Miss?" he said. I looked at him, trying to understand where I was. I looked around, and the car was sitting on the side of the highway I had been on before I had turned off. I looked around, then looked at my watch. It must have stopped. It said 8am, which was the morning.

The policeman repeated, "Is everything okay?"

"Yes, yes… I must have needed to take a nap." I blinked my eyes and shook my head, then slapped my face. "Excuse me, but… what day is it?"

When he told me the day, I said under my breath, "Impossible. How had a day passed? What in the world happened?"

After that, I spent some time at a police station, trying to convince them that I was not on drugs or crazy, although I probably needed more convincing than they did. After some tests, they let me go. I immediately drove to the place in the south central part of Ireland where I had been so many years ago, but I went straight to my hotel and decided to just hide out there for the rest of the day. I was getting scared by some of these things that were happening to me, and I felt like I was losing my grip. I knew what was real and what was imaginary, and I needed to make sure I could keep distinguishing the two. So, I stayed in the hotel room and watched some movies on TV. I ordered room service for dinner, because I was afraid of running into any other clones of blonde-haired, blue-eyed boys like the 3 I had already encountered.

I snuggled into the warm bed, and went to sleep, thankful for at least one day of normalcy.

Unfortunately, the night had different plans for me. I know it was just a dream. It was just a dream.

But in this dream, I was walking toward that little protected piece of seashore, just as Lucas and I had gone to years before. I was alone, then I felt someone holding my hand; except there was no one next to me. I came close to the waters, and gazed on them for a while. I started singing that song my grandma used to sing, "You Are My Sunshine", and after I sang that line, "Please don't take my sunshine away," I felt strong, gentle arms encircle me, and a voice say like soft honey inside my ear, "Please don't, Miss."

Then the hands lifted me up and I was inside these strong arms, and was being taken into the waters. They took me deeper, and deeper…

I struggled, as the water started to cover my face, then everything went dark.

I gasped, waking up with water choking in my throat. I thrashed about, as I felt submerged in water, then hit my head against something hard – it was the porcelain of the hotel room's bathtub. I came up from the water, and stood up, water rushing and dripping down my skin. It was morning. I had no idea what was happening to me, and I was scared.

I changed my entire plan for the trip. I didn't go anywhere near the other places I had visited before, and I avoided water. There was some strange connection to water that was warping my sense of reality, and I was just getting too old to deal with the unexpected. Once I changed my route, things calmed down. I saw some places I had missed the first time around, and was happy that I was understanding more about Ireland. I felt a little sentimental for those places I had shared with Lucas, but I understood that, as the years had passed with no communication from him, my chance of ever being reunited with him had ended. I wanted to believe in that beautiful fantasy, but the older I became the more I accepted that life is less romantic. So, I settled into a pleasant trip, even though it was disappointingly unemotional compared to my previous one.

Even though I had changed most of my itinerary, I decided to still visit Dublin, as this was one place that I had not fully seen the first time; moreover, being a city, I felt safe that nothing strange would happen there as had happened in these more remote places.

I visited various points of interest, like Trinity College, and revisited St. Patrick's cathedral. I planned to be in Dublin for just 3 days. Because of my experiences, I decided I didn't even want to drive across Ireland again like I had before, so I switched my flight to leave from Dublin.

On my second evening in Dublin, I was walking along a street and saw a guy sitting against a wall. He looked very tired and pale. He had a guitar in his lap, and was playing and singing for money. I walked up to him to listen, and all the feelings of fear came back to me. He looked a little more mature than the other 3, but this guy reminded me of the other strangers I had mysteriously met. His hair was also blonde, but a little richer in color, tending more toward a blondish honey brown; it was wavy and soft. His face was a little older, but still looked young, even though it had started to show signs of facial hair. His eyes, reflecting the weakness of his energy, were a greyish blue. I was frozen on the sidewalk. My curiosity got the better of common sense, so I listened to his weak, but attractive voice singing a song, then I put some money in his guitar case. The guy stopped singing and looked at me for a long time.

"Thank you, Miss."

"Oh, don't mention it." His voice was deeply sincere and made me feel uncomfortable, since I had only put 5 Euros I his case, barely enough for a meal. I was going to leave, but something in his eyes made me stay.

"Miss," he said, softly patting the place next to himself, "If you would, sit here a while with me."

The request was so heartfelt, I couldn't refuse. There was a pathos in his figure that made me desire to know more about him. I sat down and looked at him and his hands. They were fragile with hunger, yet still strong, and his skin was a beautifully pure white. He looked at me, and the way he looked I felt that he knew me, but this was impossible. We were strangers.

"I know what you're wondering, Miss. I'm 22 years old, although I guess deep down I'm much older. I've been waiting for a long time for someone such as you to come here and sit with me." He kept looking at me, and I felt myself being drawn into the depths of his eyes. He moved his hand over to mine, and took it with a gentleness yet a feeling of longing, for some need of connection. The touch stirred something deep inside of me, a sadness, a memory.

"Miss, you probably don't understand... I'm dying. I've been needing something for a long time. I mean, I've been needing..." The sentence trailed off, but I thought I could hear him whisper "you" at the end. But he couldn't have. He didn't know me.

He sighed. "It seems like my chances are so small now, there is just one chance. I just need you to do something. It is not so much, just a small favor."

"What is it?"

He started to caress my hand, and I felt warm inside. I began to cry, and I didn't even understand why.

"Just something small. I just need you to listen to my music."

"Listen to your music?" I pulled my hand away. Was this some kind of scam?

"Oh, Miss. Don't be so skeptical. Just..." It was hard for him to breathe. "Just... Just go and find my music. You listen to cd's, right? I think you will like this music."

I started to get up, and he grasped my arm. "Please promise me."

"Ok, ok. What is your name?"

He looked at me with a sorrow that was so inexplicable for a man who didn't know me.

"Oh, Miss. I'm hoping that you will know that soon enough."

I went back to my hotel, trying to shake this most recent experience from my mind. I didn't know how these four different guys were connected, and I felt that Ireland had some kind of strange secret that was trying to pull me in, but this was not my life. My life was across the ocean. I wouldn't let myself sleep that night – I didn't want to end up in any compromising positions, or wake up in some kind of shock.

The next day was my last day in Ireland, and I felt I probably would not return. Still, I had one more thing I had to do – I had promised that poor guy on the sidewalk that I would listen to his cd. So, the next morning I found a small music store, even though such places were disappearing as online technology was making everything irrelevant to life, and I felt my own past was becoming irrelevant. Maybe that stranger was right. I didn't know how to look at what I was seeing. I had become skeptical, and unemotional, even callous, in ways.

I looked around the shop for some kind of portable cd player and headphones and batteries, although those were slowly becoming extinct in the face of new music-listening technology. I thought about the past 15 years, and how everything had changed so quickly. Fortunately, at this little shop, many things about time had stood still, so it still had some of those artifacts of music listening technology. I picked them out, then went up to the counter.

"Will that be all for you ma'am?" the woman said.

"Well, actually, I was also looking for some music."

"No problem with that. What is the artist's name?"

"That actually is a problem. I don't know his name. It's an Irish singer, a young man… blondish brown hair."

"Do you know the age?"

"Maybe around 22 years old?" I felt very strange with this whole exchange.

The woman thought for a minute, then seemed to have an epiphany.

"Yes! He just released an album this week… It's quite good. He's 24 years old now."

She went and retrieved a cd, and brought it back to the counter. She looked at it and shook her head. "Boy, he's quite handsome… His hair used to be much blonder, and he's looking older than he did, but he's really growing into himself quite nicely."

She seemed to suddenly realize I heard her, and smiled. "Well, you'll be liking his music, too."

She gave me the cd, and I looked at the cover. My legs almost gave out from under me, and my whole body went numb. There was his face. It was the rough growth under the jaw and on the chin, the smooth skin, the wavy, honey brown hair… and those intense blue eyes. They looked at me from the picture, and I was stunned and shivering inside.

As I looked at the artist on the cd cover, I whispered the name of the man I had not seen in so many years.

Then I silently started to shed some tears.

The woman looked at me in confusion. "Ma'am? Is everything ok? Was this the one you were looking for?"

I kept looking down at his face, into those eyes, and teardrops fell on the case. I just nodded my head in silence. I thought back upon that trip 15 years ago, and every detail came back to me with mind-shattering clarity. It seemed the last moment of any normalcy ended with that first evening at the Bed and Breakfast, drinking the Irish Coffee. I thought back upon the taste of that Irish whiskey, and how it had numbed my tongue and given me my deep sleep, and then the next morning meeting this man, this Lucas, who was now staring up at me from this cd case, looking like he had not aged a day in 15 years.

"I wonder what was in that Irish Coffee," I mumbled, as I gave her the money for the purchase.

"I'm sorry, ma'am?"

"Oh, nothing. I was just thinking about how powerful Irish whiskey is."

She nodded her head vigorously as she gave me my purchase in a bag.

"Oh yes, ma'am. Irish spirits are very powerful." Then her eyes got this fearful, foreboding look that was almost comical, except she was very serious. "If you're not careful, they will overtake you."

I stared at her, and something deep within me became strong and defiant. My strong feeling was out of proportion to this conversation. Yet I said in a very serious, low voice, "What's wrong with that."

I am not sure if there was something in my eyes or in the sound of my voice, but the woman turned ashen, and backed away. After I left the shop, I could hear a little click, and as I turned around, I could see her turning the lights off inside the shop and disappearing.

I went back to my rental car, and sat there, looking at the cd. All of my things had been packed in the car, I was ready to drive to the airport. I fished inside my purse and took out the printout of my ticket. I ripped it up. But I knew the ticket wasn't enough. I took my passport out of my purse, and looked at the page with my picture and name. Something seemed wrong about this entire scenario, but I still couldn't access it. I looked at the cd and at the face staring up at me; with my fingers I traced the beauty of that visage. I looked again at my passport and sighed.

Then I tore it up.

For whatever reason, there was something deep inside of me that was telling me that I was not leaving. I would never go back to my former life again. And I had to trust that.

I knew where I had to go, and drove out to Wicklow National Forest. I left everything inside my car except this cd and cd player and headphones. I was remembering… I remembered that final night with Lucas, his gift to me, that song… *"We have already been married in heaven since many ages ago, and now on earth. I want to give you a gift as part of that. I'm going to sing you a song, in the style that you understand as a human. When I know you are ready to come back to me, you will hear me singing again… and, the spirits above and below us willing, we will be together again."*

As I walked through the forest in my bare feet, his words wracked me to the deepest part of my soul… How could I have forgotten them? I was sobbing, but I was also determined; it had been 15 years since, but I knew exactly where to go.

The place by the stream had not changed, except for one major addition – there was a fully-grown tree, towering above the rest in the forest; its trunk was massive, its branches and foliage overspreading far beyond this area. I had never seen such a tree – it seemed like a creation of the gods. As I looked at where it grew, I remembered – it was that little bud which had stuck out of the earth the last time I had been here, the place where Lucas had left me, the place where I had followed his watery departure in my dreams with my own tears upon waking.

For the first time in years, I remembered that little boy on the airplane, on my way to Ireland. His face came into my mind, then the conversation, which I had thought was strange at the time, but of no meaning.

*"I give up. What's your name?"*

*He looked very serious. "But you already know it."*

*"I'm sure I don't," I said, trying to correct the boy.*

*"You don't…" he said, seeming to ponder. "But you did."*

"You are so stupid," I said to myself. "Such a stupid, stupid human," I said, berating myself. "Nothing was ever a dream." I was starting to understand.

I looked around myself, then above to the sky, then down into the waters of the stream. "How can you ever forgive me, Lucas," I pleaded, fresh tears streaming down my face.

But I knew there was still one thing left to do.

I opened the cd case and took out the cd, and put it into the cd player. I plugged in the headphones. I turned it on, and listened. The voice was soft, and gentle and full of yearning, just like Lucas's voice had been. The singing was just like his. I kept listening to each song.

Then he started singing the title track of the album. It was the song he had sung to me so many years ago, and it tore at my emotions. Something was coming back to me, there was a well of memory that went beyond my feeble human mind, it was a deeper sense in my soul, this soul that was not part of this human shell. Then at the end of the song, the voice trailed off in a soft plea for his lover... Then I remembered his voice. Not the words, but something deeper.

I tore the headphones off of my head and threw them and the cd player into the water of the stream. They sank to bottom of the little river bed, forever destroyed. I was gasping inside myself; my human brain, with its physical limitations, was having trouble processing something... So I blocked out all my logical thoughts and went into my deepest feelings. My mouth went dry, and my hand went up to my face, as the shock sent tremors into my body. Then everything was released. I remembered who I was.

And I remembered his name.

Choking on the emotions pouring out of me, his name... My human tongue struggled with it, then I went deeper, my memory of sounds that came from somewhere beyond my human anatomy. It finally came out of me, but it was no human language that had ever been spoken, and I would never speak another word of human language again.

As soon as I said his name, I felt him behind me, his soft, strong arms encircling me. I put my hands on his arms, and held on. His honey brown hair fell in swirls, and I could feel his face against my skin as he kissed my cheek... a long, lingering kiss. He spoke in that other-worldly language, and I could understand every sense of what he said, something that human words could only feebly express...

"You came back to me, my love."

And from my inner senses, I expressed ten thousand joys, and promised that I would never leave him again.

I shed the human clothes I had been wearing, and stood against his chest, and we were pressed up against each other, our human legs entwined, his arms around me and me holding on to him. I could feel him beyond the soft skin and hair of his flesh, beyond the pulse of his human blood; there were powerful forces that this human shell could not define, which were being given back to me. I looked up into those blue human eyes for the last time, and they were the blue of the original skies and waters, before any contamination had come upon the earth. My human throat felt dry, and I could sense from him, from my lover, that soon I would never feel dry again.

We were standing on the banks near the stream, on the solid ground. He bent down and his lips pressed on mine, and he opened up every part of me… I could hear him say my name deep within my spirit, and in strong aspiration his name came out of every pore of my senses. The water from the stream started to rise, and ran more strongly; it reached our feet, then started covering the land around us. It continued to rise, and I held on to him, breathing more deeply, no longer in fear, but in expectation, in immersion, in communion… The waters rose around us completely, then the air shattered into infinite points of light… and our human bodies disappeared.

## Chapter 10: The Re-Beginning

The two had been re-joined on the banks of that stream in the place of the world called by human language Ireland. Such a love and connection had never been known by human civilization, and possibly, with their restricted minds, it would never be known. Things of the spirit and the eternal had always been within human desire, but the material, being the easiest to grasp, was what they had pursued. Thus, a love and an ecstasy such as the two lovers knew in each other was not within the imagination of humans, whose concept of love had tended toward ever smaller definitions, rather than the reverse.

So narrow had it become that the love finally imploded. The figure who had been Lucas for a short time had known of its impending nature, and had known that one chance remained for him to be joined with the mate of his own soul, although that window was so small.

Soon after their reunion, human civilization quickly pursued a path of self-destruction. The form of this destruction was irrelevant, because the end result was the most important. After several years of human time, and human chaos, there were no longer any humans left alive on earth. Then, after some more time (perhaps tens of thousands of years in the human mind), when their flesh had decayed and their bones had been used as food for the earth, not even one trace of their previous existence remained. The earth rested and regrew itself, and calmly rejoiced. Its natural music returned and reverberated in every corner of its life.

All over the earth, love was consummated and multiplied for an eternity of time, but perhaps nowhere as much so as in this place that, during one tiny period of existence, had been named Ireland, and where the ancient forests had returned more powerfully and luxuriously than before. This place was perfect for a continuous celebration of union, because it was fed on all sides by the sea, and was small enough to enjoy its intimacy. Perhaps nowhere else on earth did the love continue with a vivacity and passion as in this place, as the waters and the earth with its trees fed off of each other and played among each other; his waters fed the earth and came up into the deepest parts of her trees constantly; she felt every touch and came back by aspiration into the skies and the ensuing rains caressed him and fed his power. The rivers and streams rang with his easy laughter and brought cool, refreshing waters to the earth and trees, and she responded with gentle laughter in her boughs, and cooling shade. They were forever locked in a lovers' embrace, and the intensity of their feelings for each other was mutual and complete.

—Never the End—

Printed in Great Britain
by Amazon

23783325R00088